Where There's Smoke

Sam Vickery

For Bob, for your tenacity and because
life would be duller without you.

Chapter One

Kaitlyn

"I don't want to go."

"I know. And I wish that made a difference, darling, but it doesn't," I sighed, giving up any hope of Rex putting his own shoes and coat on and squatting down on the musty brown carpet to slide his feet into the worn school shoes. I had to loosen the laces as far as they would go to be able to prize them on his feet.

"Ouch. They're too small," he moaned, his blue eyes filling with tears that I knew had nothing to do with his footwear. I stood up, wrapping my arms around him, holding his head to my chest so he wouldn't see me holding back my own tears. His arms wrapped their way around my waist and he squeezed tightly, silently begging me to change my mind.

"Rex, we're late."

He sighed and let go of me, his head bowed as I opened the door. One small blessing about moving to our cramped, one bedroom flat was that it was on the ground floor. It meant that we had the endless noise of people coming and going directly outside the flimsy front door, but at least we didn't have to climb fifteen flights of stairs every time we came home. The lift was nothing but a dumping ground for old broken toys and crisp packets, its door wedged open in the entrance hall, a permanent invite for litter. It was horribly ironic that I often found myself back here during the course of my working day, busting my own neighbours for GBH or dealing drugs. I never stopped to chat or make small talk, conscious that I didn't want to make friends with anyone, or give them cause to recognise me. I couldn't afford to have to move again.

I shepherded Rex past the disgusting entrance hall and out onto the pavement, looking up at the thick grey clouds with trepidation. His coat was two years old now, and I knew it needed replacing. If I'd seen the state of my own child two years ago, the fraying cuffs, the yellowed collar of his shirt, I would have judged. But there was no point wasting energy on things like that now. And it wasn't as if the other kids at his school were in brand new Nikes or anything. I doubted half of them had even had breakfast. It was a far cry from the Ferraris and BMWs and designer satchels at Forest Heights prep school.

"I want you to try, today, okay? That's all I ask. Just try and speak to some of the other children – "

"They hate me, Mummy. I told you that already."

"No, they don't. They don't know you, is all. And you haven't met everyone yet. I bet there are some lovely children in your class, you just need to be brave. Ask to play."

He hung his head, kicking an empty beer can along in front of him. I tutted and put a hand out to stop him, bending down to pick it up, casting around for a bin. There was nothing. I tucked it in my handbag, hoping it didn't make everything inside stink of stale beer, realising what a wasted effort my single can was against the backdrop of bottles and packets that ran along the edges of the tower-blocks.

"They bully me, Mummy. It's not just not letting me play. I wouldn't mind that. I don't want to play with them anyway," he said bravely, though I knew he

3

was horribly lonely since moving to the new school. He stopped walking and I had to resist the urge to look down at my watch to see if we were going to be late. This was important. I made myself look at him, waiting for him to speak. His freckled cheeks reddened but he forced the words out, despite his obvious discomfort. "They try and find me. Wherever I go, they follow me. Yesterday, Oakley Withers spat in my eye. In my actual eye!"

"You didn't tell me that."

"I didn't have time to. You didn't pick me up from Sarah's until bedtime," he said, a note of accusation in his voice. "A girl called Amy took the cereal bar out of my lunch too. She said we weren't allowed to have it, but then I saw her eating it with one of her friends."

I took a breath, biting the inside of my cheek. "Did you tell a teacher?"

"They don't listen to me. They always tell me to stop making a fuss." He shrugged and I cast my eyes up to the sky, willing myself not to fall apart now. I had to keep the momentum going, to make this work.

We had no choice.

"I'll speak to Miss. Rogers. This morning."

"When? You're not even taking me in. Sarah is."

"I'll call her. Before school starts, okay? As soon as I get into work."

"It won't make any difference. I know we're poor now, since..." he shook his head and pushed his hands into his pockets, looking down the street so he didn't have to maintain eye contact with me.

I pulled him into a hug. "You don't have to be ashamed. You can say it. *Since Dad left.* It's only the truth," I said pulling back to look him in the eye. "And we're not poor. We've got a warm flat, we've got food, haven't we?"

But we're not rich anymore, are we? I had to leave my nice school. Sell my Lego, my best toys. And I never even get to see my friends anymore. I hate Dad for making us poor."

So do I, I thought silently. It had been nearly two years since Mitch had walked out on us, taking his business, his money and his new girlfriend to Dubai. I'd never believed in marriage, but in the aftermath of his leaving, realising just how far he was prepared to go not to have to pay a penny towards his tedious ex and the son he'd sired, I'd regretted my choice to live in sin bitterly. In the space of six months, we'd had to leave our beautiful home in Mayfair, moving to Brixton, the only place I'd been able to get a job and a flat we could afford with our meagre budget. I hadn't been able to scrape together the fees for Rex to keep going to his prep school, and after six years as a stay at home mum, never missing a school run, always there to read him his bedtime story and play for hours on end, I'd had to go back to the police force, taking a full-time position, accepting all the overtime I was offered and starting way back at the bottom rung again. Life had a funny way of bringing you back full circle, right back to the place you thought you'd long since escaped.

We walked in silence to the childminder's house, chosen not because she was particularly wonderful, but because she was the cheapest in the area and she didn't mind me dropping Rex off early and collecting him late. Sometimes I got stuck at work and had no choice, as much as I hated leaving him for so long. Rex kissed me goodbye without bothering to put up another protest, disappearing inside Sarah's grim terrace. I could hear the news blaring in the living room and hoped he wouldn't go in there. He had more than enough negativity to deal with, without hearing about the state of the world right now.

I was torn between feeling rclieved that he hadn't made a scene, and sad that he'd known there was no point. I turned away, sure that I was failing him, wishing not for the first time, that I hadn't put all my eggs into Mitch's basket. I should have kept working, even if only part time. I should have had my own savings, thought about the what ifs. But I'd never dreamed he would abandon us so abruptly. Looking down at my cheap market watch, I swore under my breath, before breaking into a run. I couldn't be late, not today of all days.

Chapter Two

Kaitlyn

"You're late. I was just about to call you," Marcus said, his grey moustache twitching as I rushed into the staffroom. I stripped off my jacket and grabbed a paper-towel from the dispenser beside the sink, blotting the sweat from my forehead.

"Sorry, Guv, Rex was having a tough morning," I said, checking my watch. I was two minutes late, but I already knew there was no point arguing my case with Marcus. He was a stickler for doing things properly, encouraging everyone to arrive ten minutes before their shift so that they could start work promptly.

He twisted his mouth and I hoped he wasn't about to launch into another lecture on leaving Rex to fight his own battles. For a man who had no kids of his own, he had an awful lot of opinions on how to raise them. Instead, he got straight down to business. "We have an interesting... situation."

"Oh?" I said, pouring myself a glass of water and downing it in one go, maintaining eye contact so he could see he had my attention.

"A man arrived shortly after six a.m. Big guy, built like a brick shithouse, you know the type. He wasn't making much sense to start off with, stuttering and the like. We thought he was just a drunk at first. Some guy off the streets."

"Right," I nodded, placing my glass on the draining board, wondering what this had to do with me. I really needed to call the school in the next twenty minutes if I was going to catch Rex's teacher before the kids arrived.

"He's made a confession. Well, sort of," Marcus said, scratching his cheek with his fingernail. For the guy in charge, he had a real issue with getting to the point, I thought, irritably. I couldn't understand why he was giving me all this information, rather than waiting for the team brief in five minutes. Marcus fixed me with a piercing stare. "He says his wife and baby boy are dead."

"Dead?" I repeated.

"Exactly. Dead."

"And are they?"

"Well, herein-lies the confusion. He won't speak. It's like he's gone into shock or something. He came in, guns blazing, demanding to speak to someone, got himself into a massive tizz, finally told us his wife and son are dead then clammed up completely. He hasn't even told us his name."

"Sounds like a wind up to me."

"You could be right. But we need to find out. Anyway, I thought of you."

"Me?"

"Yes. You. I think he needs a soft touch. You're a mother, aren't you? Nothing like a mother for negotiating the truth out of an unwilling party."

"I haven't done suspect interviews in years, Guv."

"No, but you want to, don't you? You've got your interview at the end of the week. I know you want that promotion. You were a Sergeant before you left the job, weren't you?"

I didn't need to answer. It was common knowledge how far I'd fallen since I'd last been in the job. I'd been heading for Inspector when I'd met Mitch, but his love for spontaneous holidays and promises to spoil me had been incompatible with my day to day life as a police Sergeant. I hated to think of how easily he'd managed to talk me out of the job now, but in my defence, living the high life in Mayfair had seemed like a fair trade at the time.

But Marcus was right. *Want* didn't even come close to the right word. I *needed* this promotion to get back on my feet. With the debts I'd been left with from Rex's school and taking out loans to afford the basics, I was barely scraping by on my salary. Getting this promotion would change everything for us. I could afford to move us out of the estate, where I lived in fear of having my door kicked in by someone putting two and two together, realising I was the constable who'd arrested their friend, their cousin, their brother. I could get us into a safer neighbourhood, a better school for Rex. Somewhere where he wouldn't be that posh, weird kid, always standing out for his differences. Somewhere he could be happy again.

I had no idea why Marcus would think of me, he'd never shown any particular interest in me before, but he had to know what this opportunity to showcase what I was capable of could mean for my prospects. If I could get to the bottom of the story, maybe even prize a confession from the guy, it could be the difference between me getting the promotion and being turned down in favour of one of the other applicants.

"Okay," I nodded. "If you just give me a moment - "

Marcus frowned, shaking his head. "A moment? With a potential murder case on our hands? We need to get moving, Kaitlyn."

He was right. Of course he was right, but I couldn't stop myself thinking of Rex, his face filled with nervous hope as he walked into his classroom, waiting for his teacher to make his day better for a change. I'd just have to call at lunchtime and hope the bullies left him to it in the meantime.

I nodded, taking a breath. "Okay," I agreed. "Where is he?"

Chapter Three

Josh
Five Years Earlier

"Honestly, I'm not in the mood, mate," I said, pausing outside the town-house, the heavy base of indistinguishable music pulsing from deep inside the building. "I've got to be at work first thing and I'd kind of planned to spend tonight with a curry and the football."

Brett laughed, slapping me hard on the shoulder. "You'd rather sit at home eating korma in your pants, than go to a house party? Come on! When was the last time you went to one of these things?"

I shrugged. "Three years ago, maybe? I'm twenty six years old, Brett. You *do* know that half the people in there are going to be drunk teenagers? You really want to be the old guy at the party?"

"It's not a teen party. I told you. It's my sister's friend. They'll all be our age, I promise. And there will be plenty of women too. It's about time you got one of your own, you know."

"Oh, look at you, six months with a girlfriend and you've gone all domesticated." I sighed heavily, knowing Brett would wear me down sooner or later. I'd known him since my first day at the fire-station, eight years ago and from day one, I'd learned one vital lesson. What Brett wants, Brett gets. It was just a matter of persistence. He could keep going until you had no resistance left in you. Nights out, a begging call on my day off to come and help him put up a shed, the frequent hopeful requests to borrow money he never seemed to pay back, despite the fact he was on a higher pay-grade than me. I could never push my will on others the way he did. It was rude, really, but I forgave him because he was generally a decent bloke and I didn't have many friends outside of work. It was good to have someone I could make plans with. But I knew our friendship relied on me going along with his plans. I *had* to give in, because that was the unspoken rule between us.

With a feeling of repressed irritation, I nodded and followed him inside the overcrowded house. The hallway was narrow and short, and habit had me casting around for the exits before I could begin to relax. Stepping into the living room, I found myself in a wide, open-plan room with big French windows at one end, flung open to a generous garden, laid in glossy black paving stones. There was a dog, a broad shouldered blue staffy, sitting with his back legs in the garden and his head in the living room, watching with interest as people passed him on their way in or out, occasionally dropping a bit of food at his paws which he gobbled up immediately.

I made up my mind to go and say hello to him. I'd always been far more comfortable with animals than I ever was with my own species, but Brett grabbed my arm, pulling me in the opposite direction towards a cackling crowd of women before I could make my escape. He dragged me right into their circle and I watched, blushing, as he confidently introduced us, grinning around at the four women as he slid a casual arm around the closest woman's waist. "So, what do you do?" she asked, leaning closer to Brett. I would have to have a quiet word with him later about respecting his girlfriend. I couldn't imagine she'd be impressed if she could see him now.

"We're firefighters," Brett grinned. "Just finished a shift."

"I bet," she replied, twisting her mouth in disbelief.

Brett pulled his iPhone from his pocket, waving it in her face and I cringed. "See," he smiled, showing her the photo of the two of us in uniform, leaning against the bright red fire engine. He held a hose under his arm, and not for the first time I held my breath, hoping he wouldn't make a joke about showing them *his* hose later. He loved the attention that came with the job. For me, even eight years on, it was something I still struggled with.

I didn't mind the children pointing and waving as we drove past. I didn't mind the old ladies who fawned over us and brought out tea and biscuits as we were packing up our equipment. But the women, the ones who changed from perfectly nice, easy going human beings, into grabby, sexually charged feral creatures the moment they got a whiff of the uniform, *they* were the ones who made my insides squirm.

It was embarrassing to be looked at like that. To have them assume I was the kind of person who had loads of one night stands and who would take them home and show them a good time. I had been brought up to treat women with respect. My mother would have killed me if I'd been the man these wild women expected me to be. I felt like I was living in the wrong time in history, really. I was a man who'd been trained to court a woman, to send flowers and pull out chairs, and pay for dinners, yet I was stuck in a world that swiped left and right and wanted to see you naked within ten minutes of meeting.

Women didn't know what to do with me. I put them off and confused them. One woman I'd taken out to dinner had told me that when I did all the things I'd been taught to do, the habits that were so ingrained in me they were as natural as breathing, I made her feel uncomfortable. She said the flowers had made her queasy. It had taken a while for me to realise that she wasn't referring to an allergy, but the gesture in itself. I made modern women sick. And so, despite the fact that my days off could be lonely, I knew there was slim hope of that changing any time soon. And I couldn't even get a dog. Not with my long shifts.

"Likes the sound of his own voice, your friend," a voice said from beside me. I turned, finding myself facing a petite, dark eyed woman with a shining bob of sable hair swinging around her narrow shoulders. I smiled uncertainly and gave a quick nod, hoping I wouldn't have to make small talk. I never knew what to say. "*You,* however, seem to have lost yours," she grinned. "What's your name?"

"Josh. Joshua Jones."

She held out a small hand and I shook it instinctively. "Franchesca," she smiled. "Or Fran if you prefer. Not Cheska."

"It's nice to meet you, Franchesca," I said, meeting her eyes for the first time. They were intense, probing and I got the feeling she was trying to figure me out. It made a change from women trying to get me to strip, which I realised with a sinking stomach was exactly what Brett was doing right now. His shirt was already half unbuttoned and I knew he'd be letting them paw him before too long. Sometimes I wondered if he'd have been happier as a stripper than a firefighter. He'd make a good waiter in the buff, it was exactly the kind of attention he loved.

I broke away from the group, desperate not to be caught up in any of that shit. There was no way I was stripping for their entertainment. "Can I get you a drink?" I asked Franchesca, manners forcing me to offer, though I really would have preferred to go and find that gorgeous staffy.

"That would be lovely," she smiled. She followed me across the room and through to the kitchen. "So, what do you do?" I asked, feeling her eyes on me.

"I'm a scientist."

"Really?"

"Yep. Stem cell research mostly."

"Wow. That sounds... hard."

She laughed. "Not really, not once you learn the ropes. I always loved science. It's fascinating to me. It kind of comes naturally, I never found it difficult to grasp." She took the glass of white wine I offered her, and took a sip. "On the other hand," she said, "I can't begin to understand how you can find the courage to walk into a burning building."

I grinned, meeting her eyes. "Well, I guess the same is true for me. It comes naturally. If someone needs help, it's instinct to give it. I could never just walk away."

"Really? Even if it put you at risk? Even though the people inside those buildings are strangers to you? Do you really care about them enough to sacrifice yourself?"

"Yes," I answered simply. "I do. If I didn't, I couldn't do the job."

She looked at me and I felt as though she was trying to read my mind. "You're an interesting man, Josh," she said finally.

"Not really."

"No, you are. I'm glad I met you." She took another sip of her wine and placed it down on the table. "Sadly, I have to go. I have an early start tomorrow." She moved to the kitchen door and I rushed to open it for her. As soon as I'd done it, I squirmed internally. Why did I always have to be the old fashioned sap who ruined everything? She looked up at me with a smile. "You're different," she said.

"Sorry, I – "

"No, I mean *good* different. I like it." She paused, a question lingering on her lips. "Look, Josh, I don't usually do this, but, would you like to go out to dinner tomorrow night? I'd like to talk to you some more."

I froze, my hand on the door frame, wondering if this was some sort of trick. How could this intelligent, beautiful woman want to spend her evening with someone like me? What could we possibly have to talk about? She was educated, a scientist for goodness sake, and I had barely scraped the grades to make it into the emergency services. She would quickly realise there wasn't much to me, and lose interest. That being said, there was something about her that fascinated me. And when was the last time anyone had asked me on a date? Propositions, yes. Wives pressing their phone-numbers into my hand while their husbands looked the other way. Offers of late night hook ups. But a date? I couldn't even remember. What did I have to lose? "Okay," I said. "That would be nice."

"Good," she nodded. "I think we're going to get on very well, Josh. I really do."

Chapter Four

Josh

The restaurant was perfect, soft music, a polite, French maître D, dim candlelit tables dotted around the delicious smelling room. I'd spent the whole day debating about how to act tonight. Whether I should try and come across as a more modern version of myself. Less fusty, as one date had labelled me. I'd practised being cool and offhand in the mirror, but I couldn't pull it off and I knew I would never be able to keep it going for more than a few minutes. Franchesca had said she liked that I was different, and since I apparently didn't have any choice in the matter, I'd resigned myself to the fact that the real me would just have to do.

I'd waited outside for Franchesca, not wanting to go in alone and appear rude. She'd been forty-five minutes late and I'd begun to think she had changed her mind, when I finally recognised her coming round the corner. She'd taken the roses I'd handed her at the door, commenting on how pretty they were and I'd felt something release inside me, some of the tension I'd been holding onto dissipating at her reaction. She hadn't squirmed when I'd held the door open for her, nor when I'd pulled out her chair. In fact, she seemed to relish the little touches. Perhaps my mother had been right all along. When I found a lady with class, I would know it because she would appreciate the things I did. A classy lady not only enjoyed them, but expected them, which was why from the age of five I'd learned to do them for my mother.

I flinched now, remembering the crack of her fist against my skull when I'd left the dinner table without her permission. The time she knocked out my front baby teeth because I'd walked into the kitchen and forgotten to hold the door open for her. She'd been meticulous in her rules, her *teachings*, she called them. She would go off on rants that lasted for hours, blasting the youth of today, lamenting the lack of manners in the young boys and girls alike. I shuddered internally, watching Franchesca now as she ate with pleasure, running over the steps in my mind, making sure I hadn't forgotten any of them.

Her water glass was almost empty and I picked up the bottle to top it up, angry at myself for not noticing sooner. I should have filled it just after the halfway point. I'd been distracted and it really wasn't good enough.

"Don't you think so?" Franchesca asked, her soft voice penetrating through my internal dialogue. I hadn't heard the question and I froze, unsure how to respond without appearing rude. "I mean, there really is something special about the French cuisine, isn't there? Have you been to Paris?"

"I haven't," I admitted. "Have you?"

"Oh yes. I try to pop over whenever I've got a long weekend. I love the culture. The atmosphere."

I nodded, feeling slow. The truth was, I hadn't seen much of England, let alone had the opportunity to pop off to France for a quick holiday. I'd barely set foot outside of London as it was. "What's it like? Paris?" I asked. "I mean, I've seen it on TV, but, what is there to do?"

"Oh, there's so much," she exclaimed with a smile. "The museums. The shopping. The *food*. I can't believe you've never been."

"I haven't had a lot of time for travel."

"Not Rome either?"

I shook my head.

"Berlin?"

"Nope. Nowhere. Sorry."

"Oh." She took a sip of wine and placed her glass down, flashing me a mischievous look. "Well," she said slowly. "We should change that. Go somewhere together. Don't you think?"

"You want to go on holiday together?" I asked in surprise.

"Am I rushing? Sorry, I tend to do that. I'm the kind of person who knows what they want and just goes right for it. Why put it off if it's something you want? Anyway, it wouldn't be a holiday. We could just go for a night. Just to give you a little taste of somewhere different."

I looked at her sparkling dark eyes, even more fascinated than I'd been when I first met her. I couldn't believe that she was interested in me. She seemed like a dream. A whirlwind of a woman who for some inexplicable reason, wanted to spend time with me.

"Say you'll come?"

"Where?"

"Paris. We can go next weekend."

I shook my head. "I can't. I'm working."

She frowned. "Surely you can get someone to cover you? Josh, it's *Paris,*" she grinned. "With *me*. You can get cover, can't you?"

"I suppose I could ask," I replied uncertainly. I wasn't sure I was ready to leave the country with her, but I had to admit, her excitement was infectious.

She sat back with a satisfied smile. "You'll figure it out. This is going to be so much fun!"

The waiter arrived with the bill and I paid immediately. Some women, in fact, most these days, offered to pay their half. Some even challenged me for the whole bill. I didn't understand it. My mother had sworn to me that a proper lady would never be so crude as to offer money towards the cost of a meal, and yet so many of them seemed nice enough in other ways. And their arguments about equality really did seem to make sense. I didn't know what to think.

Thankfully, Franchesca, stayed silent, her eyes drifting around the restaurant as I keyed in my pin-number. I was fine with that. I knew what to do and where I stood and it gave me a confidence I hadn't felt in a long time. I knew the steps to this dance and it was a relief to find myself out with a woman even my mother would have approved of.

I stood up, walking around the table to pull out her chair and helped her into her coat. She smiled graciously and I felt a buzz of excitement in my gut. This really could go somewhere. She might actually like me. I held the door so she could step outside and walked her down the street to her car. "You'll be alright getting home?"

"Yes, thank you. I've had a lovely time. You're refreshing company, Joshua Jones."

"I'm glad you enjoyed it. I did too."

She paused beside her car door, staring up at me. "Aren't you going to try and kiss me?"

I blushed, shaking my head. "I wouldn't want to make you uncomfortable."

"You won't. You couldn't." She stepped forward and I felt my hands tremble, unsure what to do. It could be a test. *A trick.* If I kissed her, she might think I was just using her, buying my way into her pants with a nice dinner, as I'd heard women say. But if I didn't, she might consider that a rejection. I could ruin everything. "Josh," she said softly, her hand on my arm. "What are you waiting for?" I looked at her smiling mouth and made my decision, lowering my face to hers and letting go of my fears.

Chapter Five

Kaitlyn

I paused in the doorway to the interview room, surprised at the sight of the person waiting inside. From Marcus's description, I'd expected something quite different from the straight backed man who sat quietly waiting at the Formica table. He held himself stiffly, like he'd spent a long time in the military or something. I'd pictured a slouched, bleary eyed, doped-up piss taker, here on a dare. Someone with nothing better to do than send us on a wild goose chase. This guy didn't fit the bill at all. His black leather jacket was pulled close around his chest, but even so, it didn't disguise his muscular build. He wore a bottle-green beany on his head, but I could see from his thick, dark eyebrows, his hair would almost certainly be dark too.

He glanced up as I came into the room, his brown eyes sweeping over my face before returning to his lap, where his hand clasped his wrist firmly, as if holding himself in check. I heard a noise and looked over my shoulder to see Marcus following close behind. *Of course* he wasn't going to leave me to do the job without coming to see the show. I should have known his trust wouldn't run that far. Ignoring him, I approached the table, wondering how best to start.

The man didn't look up as I took a seat, waiting for Marcus to settle himself beside me before I spoke. I placed my hands on the table and leaned forward. "Hello," I said, feeling like an idiot. I could almost hear Marcus's unspoken mockery about my lack of professionalism. But *he* had asked *me* to step in. He wanted me to try and lure the guy out of his stupor, and get to the bottom of his story. And I could. But only if I did it my way.

"I'm Kaitlyn. PC March."

He glanced up and I saw the struggle in his expression. He cleared his throat and nodded. "I'm Josh."

"Josh. Lovely. What's your last name, Josh?" He shook his head and I followed his cue. "Can you tell me why you've come in today, Josh?"

"I – didn't they tell you?" he asked softly.

"There seems to be a bit of confusion over what's actually happened. I'd like it if *you* could tell me what's going on?"

His eyes flicked to Marcus, then back to his lap. His whole body seemed to curl in on itself, his broad shoulders rounding, his head dipping low. I wished I could ask Marcus to give us a few minutes alone. He was emitting that irritating buzz of judgement and impatience that came naturally to him, and I was sure Josh could feel it too. I lowered my voice, speaking softly. "Josh, you can tell me. We can't help you if we don't know what's going on, can we?" I said, reminded of a thousand similar conversations I'd had with Rex lately. An image of my sweet eight year old son burned bright in my mind. I hoped he was okay. That he'd found the courage to approach some children and been accepted by them for once. I swallowed, blinking back the picture of his tear-stained face, focusing on the man in front of me. I could see the shadow of a bruise running beneath his eye, but decided not to bring it up just yet. "Josh?" I pushed.

He raised his head and I saw with surprise that tears were flowing down his cheeks. He made no attempt to lift his hand and wipe them away. "They're dead," he said, his voice barely a whisper. "I came as soon as I could. I came straight here, but..." he gave a juddering sigh that made my throat constrict tightly in empathy. "I can't do this. It's too hard to talk about. I'm sorry, I didn't realise how difficult this would be."

"Josh, tell me who's dead."

He stared at me, his eyes wide, filled with an unspoken agony. "My son," he choked. "My sweet, tiny baby boy. And my wife."

I glanced at Marcus who was tapping his pen rapidly against his knee, his eyes bright with agitation as he struggled with his obvious urge to interrupt. "What happened to them, Josh? How did they die?"

He shook his head. "I can't... I can't talk about it, not yet," he whispered.

"Where are they, Josh? At your home?" He nodded. "Okay." I took a breath, my thoughts running at a thousand miles an hour. "Okay," I repeated, trying to keep my breathing under control.

This was big. If he was telling the truth, it would be big. I flipped open my laptop and fixed Josh with a determined stare. "Tell me your address, Josh. We need to go to your home, now," I insisted, using the same tone I saved for when Rex wouldn't go to bed. It worked.

Josh gave a nod of defeat and put his head in his hands. Then, he took a deep breath and told me.

Marcus was back in control the moment we left the room, ordering people around, one guy to take Josh to a cell while we figured out what was going on, another pair to drive over to the address he'd given and confirm his story. I followed behind him, my heart thumping hard against my ribs. "Do you think he killed them?" I asked as Marcus spun to face me. "I mean, he didn't seem to know what was going on, did he? It's like he's in shock or something."

"We don't even know if what he's told us is true yet. Let's wait and see, shall we? If his wife and son really are dead, we'll know in the next fifteen minutes."

I nodded, my mouth dry as I thought about what would come next. "Guv, if... I mean, if they are dead... can I..." I shook my head, starting again. "I would like to continue questioning him," I said, holding my head high. "I feel like I can get him to talk."

Marcus fixed me with a penetrating stare. "Let's wait and see," he repeated. He reached forward, placing a hand on my shoulder, his expression softening. "But I don't see why not. As long as I'm in there with you, I'm happy to let you continue. I just hope you won't have to," he sighed. He squeezed my shoulder and let go, turning to look out of the window. The storm had broken whilst we'd been in the interview room and heavy rain pelted against the glass, condensation forming on the inside, trickling down in tiny rivulets. I excused myself from his office and rushed through the station towards the front entrance, jogging through the relentless rain towards the smoking shelter across the car-park. I didn't fancy an audience while I discussed my son's current situation with his teacher. Plucking my phone from my pocket, I caught sight of the time. If I called now,

I might catch Miss. Rogers during the children's lunch break, though from experience, I knew she would be less than empathetic about Rex's struggles.

I tapped my foot impatiently as the phone rang and rang, before the echoey sounds of the answerphone message kicked in, the receptionist, Mrs. Simms' halting voice asking me to leave a message after the tone. I hung up and tried again with the same result, watching the door of the station nervously. I was just about to cut the call and try a third time when Marcus appeared in the doorway, gesticulating impatiently for me to come back. I held up a hand, deciding to leave a message after-all. It was better than doing nothing. "Hi, this is Kaitlyn March, Rex's mummy. I really need to have a chat with Miss. Rogers about some struggles he's been having. Please, can you ask her to call me back as soon as possible, it's rather urgent." I rattled off my mobile number, nodding in Marcus's direction to stop him from turning purple in his impatience with me, then hung up, running towards him with nervous anticipation. I came to a halt in front of him. "Sorry, I – "

He held up a hand cutting me off mid-sentence. "They've found the wife," he said grimly.

"And?"

"Dead."

"Oh. Right."

"Looks like a single stab wound to the belly. They found her collapsed in the hallway and the rest of the house is in a mess apparently," he said.

"And the baby?" I asked, half wishing I didn't have to hear the answer.

Marcus shook his head. "They've searched the whole place. There's no baby. This chap of ours has some serious questions to answer, whether he's ready to talk, or not."

Chapter Six

Josh

"What do you mean you can't come? I've already packed!" Franchesca's angry voice echoed down the phone-line. "You said you would sort it!"

"I said I'd try. And I did manage to get cover," I told her, squeezing my eyes shut at the sound of disapproval in her voice. I hated that I'd caused her to be upset. "I have the weekend off. I just didn't realise it would take so long to get a passport. I thought it would be easy to do. I'm really sorry, Franchesca."

"What kind of grown man doesn't have a passport?" she snapped.

The kind who has never left his home city, I thought wryly. The kind who never had an opportunity to go away until now. Still, I wished I'd thought of this before. I really should have got one sooner, she was right. I shouldn't have let her get her hopes up. "I'm sorry to spoil our plans. I've put in the paperwork now, so maybe in a couple of months, we can do it then? We could still do something this weekend? I thought you might like to go for lunch? And we could go to the theatre too? Let me make it up to you?"

There was a long pause and then she sighed. "I don't think so, Josh. Maybe some other time." She hung up the phone and I stared at the black screen, furious at myself for having ruined everything. If there was ever a woman who was going to appreciate the things I did, the quirks I couldn't seem to rid myself of, it would have been her. She was the first person who'd actually seemed to like me for who I was, despite our polar opposite lifestyles. It was my chance, and I had ruined it.

I leaned against the wall, listening to the sounds of the guys in the kitchen, eating their way through a pot of stew. I was glad I hadn't mentioned my date to them. I didn't think I could cope with the jokes at my expense now that it was all over. I dropped my phone on the table with a sigh, just as the alarm sounded, reverberating through the station, piercing through the quiet, my body jumping instantly into action.

I ran out of the room, down the hall, sliding

down the pole, my feet carrying me towards the fire-engine the second I hit the ground. Brett was shouting instructions as I yanked on my turnout gear and jumped into the driver's seat, glad to have something to focus on, to take my mind off the uncomfortable conversation with Fran. The siren blared as we sped out into the busy midday traffic, heading towards the source of the call. A block of flats in the middle of Nightingale estate, fifth floor. My heart sank as I pictured the address. Flats were right at the top of my list when it came to my least favourite places to be called out to.

I glanced in my mirror, relieved to see Dave speeding close behind me, and Rebecca in a third engine not far behind him. You couldn't be too careful when it came to these situations. We might need all hands on deck. I swore under my breath as a woman tried to cut across the road ahead of us, my instincts torn between the chivalry of letting her cross, and the emergency she was delaying us from reaching. Brett reached across, beeping the horn aggressively and she jumped back flipping us the finger. "Bet she wouldn't be such a cow if it was her mother's house on fire, would she?" Brett said wryly.

I rounded the corner, and drove as fast as I could manage through the maze of narrow roads, Barry shouting directions as I zigged and zagged deeper into the estate. A group of kids ran alongside us, calling and whistling as we shot past them and I saw the excitement in their faces, remembering how I'd felt all those years back, waiting for my heroes to drive past me.

There was mercifully no sign of smoke in the direction of the flats and as we pulled up on the road outside, there were none of the signs of panic I'd feared we would find. Two women stood smoking in their dressing gowns on one of the first floor balconies, and when they saw us, they leaned over the side, whistling and shouting from above in the way that always made me feel sick. It was so damn disrespectful. I couldn't help but wonder if they'd both stayed in their dressing gowns all day, or if they'd just changed back into them the moment they got home from work or the school run. My mother would have turned in her grave at the idea of being seen in her night clothes indoors, let alone out in the open like these women. I turned away, focusing on the job.

"What do we know?" I asked Mike, the captain, as he jumped out of Rebecca's engine and strode purposefully towards the building.

"Fuck all. The call got cut off after they got the address and we haven't been able to get back through to whoever rang. All we know is that there's a fire in the kitchen. But where the hell *is* everyone? And why is the alarm not sounding?" he yelled, looking around at the perfectly ordinary situation we'd arrived at. "No sign of smoke. I swear, if this is another hoax – "

"Let's get in there and find out," Brett said. Mike nodded and we split into teams. I headed inside with Brett, Rebecca, Mike and Laurence, locating the stairs easily and jogging up them two at a time. It didn't make sense. If it were a fire, people would be getting out. People would be talking about it. And why wasn't the alarm going off? I concentrated on moving up and up, my breath quickening beneath the bulk of my bunker gear. I felt a trickle of sweat run between my shoulder-blades, itchy and out of reach. We got to door number 157, the source of the call and Mike pounded on it with his fists. "Fire service," he yelled. "Open up."

The neighbour from one flat down opened his door, stepping into the hall. He was a scrawny lad of about twenty years old, his arms covered in bright tattoos, his feet dirty and bare. He frowned in my direction. "Wos' goin' on, mate?"

"We've had reports of a fire in this building. Have you seen or heard anything?" I said.

"Nah. But the woman who lives in there is a right nut job. I'll bet she's winding you up."

"She better not be," Brett growled. "There are three engines out because of that call." Mike banged on the door again and waited.

"There's no sound of anyone in there. Do you think it's a hoax?" Rebecca frowned.

Mike shook his head. "Something's off. I want to get inside. Josh, you do the honours."

I nodded, glad to be of help. Leaning back, I

swung my leg forward, slamming the sole of my boot into the centre of the door. It crashed open and the five of us stood at the threshold, staring inside.

"Shit. Do you smell that?" Mike said, raising his forearm to cover his face. "Carbon monoxide."

"What? You can't smell carbon monoxide, can you?" Rebecca asked, peering inside the doorway.

"Actually, *I* can. Call it a gift, but you can take my word for it."

"He's right," Brett said. "It's not the CO, it's the associated gasses that give off the smell. Combustion by-products. Some people are more sensitive to noticing them, but there's a good chance that CO is present too. Mike's been right on this before."

"And I'm right now. I'd put money on it. So let's not waste time, okay?" Mike said gruffly. "Smoke hoods on everyone. Rebecca, get on the radio, get the guys on the job of evacuating the building straight away. Locate the alarm and set it off for Christ sake. Sir, you need to go outside," Mike called to the tattoo covered lad. "Right now!"

I knew Mike well enough to take his word for it. I

would trust the guy with my life, and *had* on so many occasions I'd lost count. If he said there was carbon monoxide, then I believed him. I pulled my smoke hood over my head. It wasn't perfect, but it would give us about fifteen minutes, enough time to find out what was going on. Brett and Mike pushed through the door, Laurence and I close behind. They fanned out, Mike heading to the kitchen, Brett making for the living room. I went into the bedroom.

The curtains were drawn and the bed unmade. I walked around it and there, sprawled on the carpet was a woman in a floral knee length dress, her grey hair loose around her face. She was clearly unconscious. I scooped her up easily and carried her out of the room, signalling to Mike who was emerging from the kitchen. He gave the thumbs up and I carried her out of the flat, hitching her over my shoulder as I moved as fast as I could manage down the stairs and into the blissful fresh air outside. Two ambulances were standing by and I laid her on the grass and stood back, the paramedics already rushing forward to take over.

I pulled the smoke hood from my face and took a deep breath of clean fresh air, watching the doors for the rest of the team. The residents were crowded onto the pavements now, spilling out into the road, talking loudly, arguing and laughing and begging cigarettes from each other. A cough came from behind me and I turned to see the flickering eyes of the woman I'd carried out.

"Will she be okay?" I asked the closest paramedic as they lifted her onto a stretcher and wheeled her past me towards the open doors of the waiting ambulance.

"I think so. But ten more minutes and it would have been a different story. Well done," he said.

"You too." We exchanged a nod of mutual respect and he hopped into the driver's seat of the ambulance, starting it up the second the door slammed shut, speeding off with sirens blaring. A voice came from behind me and I turned in relief to find the rest of my team emerging through the double doors.

"Boiler," Mike said, yanking his mask from his

face. It's new, the sticker on it said it was fitted three days ago and it's a fucking cowboy job. Piss poor. I think my six year old could have made better work of it," he said, anger making his voice tremble. I knew he was only so worked up because he, like the rest of us, was thinking about the consequences if we hadn't caught it in time. The lives that could have been lost. "The levels are stupidly high. This lot won't be able to go back in until it's dissipated," he said, gesturing to the crowd who were craning their necks to see the action. "I've turned off the gas and the rest is up to the gas emergency services."

"I still don't get why she called us?" I said, looking up at the fifteen story building, relieved that it hadn't been a fire after all. It could have been so much worse.

Rebecca patted my shoulder, and I saw the same confusion on her face. "I guess she must have realised something was wrong," she shrugged. "She should have at least opened a window, though. Who knows *what* she was thinking!"

"I do," Laurence said, coming to stand beside us.

He held up a fat journal and opened it to show us the scrawling handwriting inside. "Found this on the table, open here." He flicked through it, and read aloud. "The title," he grinned, "is *'How to find a husband,'* and there are several motivational bullet-points below it, on remembering to apply your lipstick well and choosing a flattering outfit."

"What has this got to do with us?" I asked.

"Ahem," Laurence coughed, smiling as he held up the journal to read again. *"Monday, book an emergency appointment to the GP and make sure it's Dr. Clarence, not that ugly one. Come up with something urgent but not off putting, ideally that I need to remove clothes for."*

"What the – " Mike exclaimed.

"Tuesday," Laurence interrupted. *"Approach Waitrose manager to compliment a staff member and ask for a date. Wednesday, call out firemen and wait to be rescued."* He looked up, shaking his head in disgust. "Looks like we were all part of her big plan. I think the gas was just a terrible, or very fortunate coincidence."

"Wow," Rebecca said, shaking her head. "I wonder which one of you she'd have worked her magic on. Josh, you've been single so long you might have actually fallen for her charms."

"Thanks, Bex. Thanks a lot," I said, trying to keep my voice light as my thoughts returned to Franchesca.

"For fuck sake," Mike breathed, with a look of barely concealed fury on his lined face. "I'm glad the gas was there or I'd *really* be livid. What a stupid thing to do!" He grabbed his smoke mask from where he'd tossed it on the grass. "Come on you lot, we'd better get back to the station. You know, in case there's an actual fire or something," he smirked.

We traipsed back to the fire-engines, leaving one of the three behind with a handful of the team to keep things in order until it was safe for the residents to go back in. The drive back to the station was quiet, all of us lost in our own thoughts, the after effects of the adrenaline that came with every emergency call out. We got back as the sun was beginning to set and I went upstairs, picking up my phone from the table where I'd left it. A blue light flashed on the screen and I keyed in my pin code, reading the text message. It was *her!*

On second thoughts, the theatre sounds lovely. We can go to that new Michelin star restaurant on Kevant Street beforehand. See you Saturday, don't let me down, F

I punched the air triumphantly. I'd been given a second chance and I was going to make absolutely sure I didn't waste it. If she wanted Michelin star food, that was exactly what she'd get. It was no more than she deserved.

Chapter Seven

Kaitlyn

"We've got a problem, Guv," Max said as Marcus and I went back inside the station.

"Oh?" Marcus replied, raising an eyebrow at the young PC.

"This fella, Josh. He's hurt."

"Since when?"

Max glanced uneasily in my direction and I waited for him to offer up an answer. "Didn't you see the state of the bloke? We took his hat and jacket so we could put him in the cell, like you said, Guv. You can't miss it. He's been messed up bad. Pretty sure his wrist is broken. His head is all bloodied up too."

"You're joking?" Marcus said, looking from Max to me. "Did you notice, Kaitlyn?"

I shrugged. "He had a bruise by his eye, but other than that I didn't see anything to write home about. He *was* pretty well covered though."

Max stepped closer, lowering his voice. "Do you think they got into a fight? His wife and him, I mean?"

"Never mind how it happened. What have you done with him?" Marcus said, folding his arms across his chest.

Max shrugged. "I put him in the cell, like you said. But I think he needs to go to hospital."

Marcus looked at me. "Not before we ask him some questions."

"Are you sure that's a good idea?" I asked, screwing up my face. "I mean, if it's as bad as Max says – "

"If it were, he'd have asked to go to hospital himself, wouldn't he?" Marcus reasoned. "Did you check his wallet? Find a name?"

Max nodded. "Yep, Joshua Jones. And there was also this," he said, holding out an I.D card.

Marcus raised an eyebrow. "Fire brigade? He's a bloody firefighter?" he exclaimed, confusion flashing across his features.

"That doesn't mean he didn't do it," I pointed out. "You never know what goes on behind closed doors. We need to keep an open mind here," I said, though the information had thrown me too.

Marcus gave a short nod and I could see he was irritated by my unsolicited advice. He took the I.D card from Max and slipped it into his pocket. "Bring him to room six and we'll assess the damage for ourselves," he barked at Max. "Kaitlyn, you come with me."

Max nodded and disappeared off towards the holding cells, leaving me to follow behind Marcus. He entered the interview room briskly and pulled out a chair, gesturing for me to do the same. "You need to get some answers out of this guy, Kait, and fast. The team at the house said there's plenty of evidence of a baby having lived there up until very recently. No photos of him, but bottles, a cot... Josh isn't lying about that, at least. But we need to know where the child is. If there's any chance we can save this baby, we need to move fast."

I nodded feeling suddenly way out of my depth. "Should I maybe sit back and let you do the talking this time, Guv?"

Marcus glared at me. "Don't you dare get the

jitters on me now. I'm going out on a limb as it is to give you this chance. You want to prove you're capable of the job, don't you? Have something to tell the panel on Friday?"

"Yes," I nodded. "I do."

"So get on with it." He folded his arms tightly across his chest, his moustache twitching as he pursed his lips. I couldn't decide if he was doing this as some kind of punishment or if he actually *wanted* me to succeed. He'd never shown any sign that he cared either way about my success or failures. It was easy to tell myself he must have seen something in my work, some potential that deserved to be utilised, but he could have just as easily been doing it to show me I wasn't up to the job.

I tried to remember if I'd done anything that might have annoyed him recently. There had been the time he'd yelled at me over not catching the teenaged boy who'd thrown a brick through a window right in front of me, but as willing as I was to give the job my all, I couldn't match the speed of the moped that had pulled up alongside him and sped off before I could get my hands on the yob. Besides, I knew better than to put too much thought into a case like that. They were ten a penny. Marcus had just been letting off steam.

Whatever his reason for choosing me to assist on this case, he was right about one thing. There would never be a better way of proving I could be a decent Sergeant than getting a confession out of a murder suspect. The thought jolted me. Were we really about to discover this was a murder case? Could this polite, softly spoken gentleman who'd been unable to snub my introduction, really have killed his wife? His *baby?* The thought made my stomach twist uncomfortably.

The sound of slow footsteps grew louder as Max brought him in to us, and pointed in the direction of the seat. Now that he wasn't in his hat and jacket, it was easy to see the real state he was in. He used his left hand to pull back the chair and I caught Marcus's eye as we both clocked the swollen, purple skin around his right wrist. Without the hat, I could confirm that his hair was indeed dark, cropped military short but also distinctly matted with clumps of dried blood. His ear was crusted with dried blood and he scratched at it with a fingernail as he took his seat opposite us.

"Josh, you're hurt," I said, peering into his face, trying to get him to meet my eyes. "Why didn't you mention it?"

He shrugged, looking down at his wrist as if it were inconsequential to the situation. He placed his hands in his lap and looked up at me. "Did you find her? My wife?"

I resisted the urge to break eye contact, holding his gaze as I watched for some clue, a flash of guilt or anger at the mention of her. There was a sense of urgency in the way he spoke. "Yes," I answered softly. "The team found your wife." I paused, willing him to speak, to deny his guilt. He continued to stare at me, waiting.

"Was she dead?" he asked, his eyes boring into mine.

"She was. As I'm sure you already know."

He sighed, a shuddering, guttural sound, his shoulders slumping as he looked down at his lap. "So it's over," he whispered, more to himself than to me.

"I'd say, it's just beginning. Tell me what happened. How did your wife end up with a fatal knife wound in the early hours of this morning, Josh?" He ignored my question, his head tilted low towards his lap. "Okay." I glanced at Marcus and he gave a short nod. "Mr. Jones, where is your baby?"

His head snapped up, the numb, blank features replaced instantly with an expression that made me sit back in my chair, the pain in his eyes alive with an intensity I could hardly stand to look at. "He – I," he stuttered. He glanced towards the door of the interview room, then squeezed his eyes tightly shut. When he finally opened them again, his features were smooth and unreadable once again. "I don't know," he whispered.

"I find that hard to believe." I leaned closer, ready to go in for the kill. "Did you kill your wife and your son, Mr. Jones?"

"What?"

"You heard me. You admitted yourself that your wife and son were dead. Your neighbours have heard nothing, there's no sign of a break in and you look like you've been in one hell of a fight. Did you go out? Have a few drinks and get yourself into a scrap at the pub? Come home and take some of that aggression out on your family? *Your baby?*" I said, aware that my voice was growing steadily louder. "Did you kill them, Josh? Did you?"

"Stop!" he yelled, slamming his hand down on the table, the sound reverberating around the room. "Please, stop!"

I sat back, shaken by my own outburst. I hadn't meant to let things get so heated, so aggressive. But when I pictured a tiny baby dying at the hands of a fully grown man, it made me sick to my stomach. It made me think of what I would do if someone tried to hurt Rex. How Josh's wife must have felt in her final moments. I was making assumptions. Jumping to conclusions far too soon and that was not the professional, capable approach I needed to take. I took a deep breath, then another before speaking again. "We need to find your son, do you understand, Mr. Jones? We *have to* know where he is."

"I don't know," Josh said, his shoulders slumping. "I can't tell you."

My cheeks burned hotly, and I knew without having to look that I was flushed with anger. I needed to get a grip if I was going to make any progress. I leaned back, breathing slowly through my nostrils, then fixed him with an unwavering stare. "Did – "

"Let's stop there," Marcus interrupted, placing an unexpected hand on my forearm with unspoken authority. "Mr. Jones, you are by no means free to go, but you're clearly in need of medical attention. You'll be escorted to hospital for treatment and brought back here immediately afterwards to continue questioning. In the meantime, if you feel that you would like to cooperate and pass on any information that can help us locate your son, I would strongly encourage it," he said with a deep frown. He stood up without so much as glancing at me and left the room, leaving me to stare open mouthed after him.

"I didn't lose control," I argued, seething as I tossed two teabags into the chipped mugs in front of me. I sloshed hot water and milk into the cups and stirred the bags viciously.

"That's not what I said. But you were clearly upset. I thought it best to take a break before continuing," Marcus said, holding out his hand for his tea. I passed it to him, not meeting his eyes.

"But *he* was getting upset too, Guv. People talk when they're worked up. You know that."

"Do you think he did it?"

"I don't know," I admitted. "But we have a dead woman and a missing child who is more than likely dead too, judging by what he's told us. And now we have no suspect to question!"

Marcus prized open the scratched black tin on the table, dipping his hand into it and pulling out a bourbon. He lowered it into his mug and I cringed as he lifted the soggy brown biscuit to his quivering moustache. He spoke through a mouthful of crumbs. "He'll be back. Besides, you were the one who said it was wrong to question him before he saw a doctor," he pointed out. "It's done. No point going over it again." He leaned back in his chair folding his arms casually across his belly. "So, do you want to hear the case updates, or not?"

I bit back a sarcastic retort and nodded. "Yes. What do we know?"

"I just got off the phone with Jimmy. Forensics have arrived at the house and interviews of the neighbours have continued. Seems the wife liked to keep herself to herself. The word *antisocial* was used by more than one of them. Here's the funny thing though. They all had nothing but positive words for our Mr. Jones. On paper, he's the perfect neighbour, always up for a chat at the garden gate, popping round to help with a burst pipe. One old dear even said he'd frequently carried her shopping in from the car and unpacked it for her."

"You're joking?"

He shook his head. "But out of the seven neighbours the team visited, not a single one could remember having seen either of them in the past month. And all except two didn't even know they'd had a baby."

I shrugged. "That's not that unusual. Lots of

mums lie low for the first month or so after having a baby," I said, thinking of the first few blissful weeks I'd had with Rex, when my biggest worry had been whether to watch *Loose Women* or *Escape to the country,* whilst cuddling up in bed with him. I didn't want to remember how sweet Mitch had been back then, how he'd insisted we take it easy, bringing me hot drinks and snacks, calling several times a day from work to make sure we were comfortable. He'd led us into a false sense of security, acting as if he'd always take care of us. Pretending he cared, before getting bored and moving on to more interesting pastures. I swallowed back the rage that his name always came with and took a sip of my tea, burning my tongue in the process. I looked up, realising Marcus was still talking.

"... out at the moment searching for the baby. The sooner we find him, the better. Now that Josh is otherwise occupied, I'm going to make use of the time and head over to the house. You'll come with me," he said, a statement more than a question. My phone rang before I could give an answer and I held up a finger as I saw the number for Rex's school flash across the screen. "One moment, Guv, I need to take this, it's urgent." I didn't wait for him to protest as I stepped out of the room, pressing the phone to my ear.

"Yes, hello?"

"Miss. March?"

"Yes, speaking."

"This is Miss. Rogers."

"Oh good, you got my message? I was hoping – "

"I'm sorry, I haven't had chance to go through my messages yet. I'm afraid we've had an incident during lunch."

"Oh, I see," I said, not understanding what that had to do with me.

"I'm afraid Rex was caught fighting, Miss. March."

"Excuse me?"

"Your son was involved in a fight, in the playground. I'm afraid he lost."

"Lost?" I repeated. "What the hell does that mean?" I heard the unmistakable sound of a long, drawn out sigh, a sound of utter apathy from

someone who'd long since given up any hope of making a difference in the world. It was hard to grasp how a young teacher, a woman not more than a couple of years out of university, could already be so jaded, so uninterested in the children she was charged with educating. For a split second, I wanted to reach down the phone-line and slap her face for letting my son come to harm. "Rex wouldn't have started a fight. He would have been defending himself. He'd never go looking for trouble!"

"As you can imagine, every parent I speak to tells me the very same thing."

"Is he okay?"

"He'll live. But he's refusing to leave the playground and come inside. He's made a hell of a scene, actually. You'll have to come and get him."

"You've left him outside?"

"There's a T.A watching him."

There was so much I wanted to say to her, but it wasn't the time. Rex was hurt and scared and he needed me. That was all that mattered now. "I'll be there in thirty minutes. Please, tell him I'm coming."

"I *do* have other children who are actually willing to learn, Miss. March. I really don't have time to pander children who choose to get themselves into trouble." She hung up without waiting for a reply and I realised I was shaking with a combined sense of rage and fear. I looked up to find Marcus staring at me.

"Ready?" he asked, handing me my coat.

I shook my head. "I can't come. I need to get to the school. Rex has been hurt."

"Hurt?"

"He's been having trouble with some bullies," I confessed. "And now, it looks like he's been beaten up." I yanked my arms into my coat, blinking back the tears.

"And you think mummy rushing in to save him is going to fix the issue? He won't learn to stand up for himself if you're always there to save him, will he?"

"Marcus, he's hurt. I don't even know how badly."

"If it was that bad, *we'd* have been called, wouldn't we?" he said.

The thought made me stop in my tracks. He was

right. This time, it might have only been a few punches and kicks. Some harsh words. It was bad enough, especially when I knew Rex would never have done anything to rile them up. But what if next time it was worse? What if the next call was to tell me he'd been stabbed? Shot?

The kids he went to school with came from families where carrying weapons was the norm. The old threat of *I'll set my big brother on you,* meant a whole lot more these days than it had when I was growing up. Things escalated from nought to sixty in the blink of an eye, and I'd seen younger and younger victims of knife crime in the city since coming back to the job.

I fixed Marcus with a determined stare. "My son is hurt," I repeated. "I'm sorry if that's not convenient, but I'm going to collect him now."

Marcus pursed his lips, the colour blanching from them. He gave a short nod and turned away. "Be back here first thing tomorrow morning, or I'll get someone else to take your place," he called over his shoulder as he walked down the corridor.

"I will," I said, wondering how on earth I was going to manage to keep my word. Somehow, I would have to find a way.

Chapter Eight

Kaitlyn

I eased my way out of the lumpy single bed, careful not to wake Rex as I slid my arm out from beneath his sweat dampened head and stood up. Pulling his Lego Ninjago duvet cover to his shoulders, I stared down at his silky eyelashes fanned against his freckled cheeks and wondered how I could protect him from this new, harsh life we'd been dropped into.

He had been shaking with fear when I'd rushed onto the playground, only to discover him sitting on the wall furthest from the school building, his whole body curled into itself, his arms wrapped around his head to block out the noise of the teaching assistant who was shouting insults and threats at him. She'd turned to me with no trace of guilt at being caught laying into a terrified small boy, merely tutting as I ran to him, before telling me his behaviour was out of control.

Rex had melted into my arms with such intense relief that I hadn't even bothered to tell her how very mistaken she was. I'd just carried him to the car and brought him straight home, feeding him hot chocolate and toasted cheese sandwiches in bed, then holding him as he sobbed, trying not to throw up at the thought of what I'd put him through.

He spoke through choking sobs, explaining what had happened, his fists curled tightly around my forearm as if to keep me from leaving. Oakley Withers and two other boys from his class had spent the morning teasing him with increasing viciousness, first kicking him under the table, then scribbling on his English work. He'd asked Miss. Rogers if he could move to another table, but she'd shouted at him too, telling him to stop making a fuss. After that, no doubt seeing there would be no consequences to their bullying, their efforts had escalated and Rex had been too afraid to ask for help again.

They'd snapped his new Star Wars pencil. Scratched his arms. Pinched his legs under the table. Called him *'posh twat'* and *'bum boy,'* though he had no idea what any of the words meant. At lunch, he'd tried to take as long as he could over his sandwich in the dining hall, so that he wouldn't be sent out to the playground. But the dinner lady had yelled at him for messing around and thrown his food in the bin, shoving him out the door onto the playground. It had only taken a few minutes for the little gang of boys to discover his hiding place behind the bins. He'd tried to run, but they were too quick, too determined.

He'd looked up at me with wide, round eyes as he spoke. "So, I just laid there as still as I could, and wished they would stop hitting me."

I'd wanted so much to promise that he'd never have to go back to that place. That I would protect him. But how could I? I *had to* work. It was the only way to keep a roof over our heads and food on the table.

I slipped out of the bedroom now and padded downstairs, my whole body aching with the effort of holding in my emotions all afternoon. Flicking the switch on the kettle, I pushed the last morsel of Rex's toastie into my mouth, hoping it would tide me over until breakfast. It would have to. I brewed a pot of tea in lieu of dinner and took it into the cramped living room, trying to ignore the ugly nicotine stained wallpaper and worn brown carpet. I wanted my mum. I wanted her to tell me I wasn't a complete failure, and that she'd had these moments too whilst raising me. It had been so long since we'd made the trip to Pembrokeshire, back to the tiny village where I'd grown up, so safe and free. So different from the life Rex was living.

I poured a mug of tea from the burgundy pot and picked up the handset of the old-fashioned rotary telephone, meticulously dialling the phone-number that I'd known since I was seven. It wasn't yet nine p.m. and I knew my mother would still be up, a fire roaring in the stone hearth, ever present no matter the season, a cat on her lap, another warming her feet as she watched nature documentaries and worked on embroidered nightgowns to sell at the local arts and crafts shop. Her voice was instantly soothing as she answered and I closed my eyes, determined not to cry and make her worry. It wasn't her job to rescue me.

"Mum?"

"Oh, Kaity, what a lovely surprise, how are you,

sweetheart?"

And that was all it took. My strength dissolved into a puddle of tears as I relayed the whole story of what had been going on with Rex, my fears over not getting the promotion, even the potential murder case that had been dropped in my lap this morning.

"And the baby's still missing, Mum, and I'm so afraid I'm going to mess everything up. I miss my old life," I admitted, wiping roughly at my eyes. "I hate Mitch for what he did, but if it would keep Rex from having to go through this daily torture, I'd take him back in a heartbeat."

"No, Kait, it would make you miserable. A man like that doesn't deserve you."

"And Rex doesn't deserve this."

"Are you happy? In your work? Your life? You still haven't let me come and visit your flat. I worry about you."

I sighed. "Police work isn't what it was when I left to have Rex, you know? The funding cuts have meant that we're stretched tighter than ever, and the paperwork is pretty overwhelming. And, it's *London*. It was never going to be dolling out slaps on the wrist for underage drinking. I worry too. I'm scared of what will happen to Rex if I'm not around." I didn't want to admit out loud that I had a reoccurring nightmare about being shot whilst trying to break up a fight. I wished I could brush it off as silly, just my overactive imagination creating worries out of nothing, but the truth was, these days it was a real possibility.

I heard Mum sigh, and waited. "I would never have said anything, sweetheart, because it's not my place. You're a grown woman and you've had to make some tough choices over the last few years. But knowing that you're struggling so much..." she paused and I swallowed hard against the lump that had formed in my throat. "I think you should come home. There's a job going at the local station, Joanna was telling me just this morning. It's not as exciting as working in the capital, but it's a damn sight safer. Little Rex could go to the primary in the village. Sue Maddox is the head there now, you remember her?"

"I do," I nodded tearfully. Sue was a few years

older than me and growing up, I'd played out in the fields with her and her brothers after school. She'd been a kind, softly spoken girl who always looked out for the little ones and broke up disagreements in a calm, fair manner. She had that special something that made all the children stop and pay attention to her, whilst still managing to be universally liked. In short, she was exactly the kind of person you'd want to take care of your child in your absence. I gave a wry laugh. "You make it sound so idyllic, Mum. But I can't come home."

"Why not? Because you'd consider it a failure? Worry what everyone would have to say about it?" she said perceptively. I knew she was picturing the smug expression on my face when I'd told everyone at the local pub that I was moving to London to join the police force. When I'd moved in with Mitch, I'd sent home a photo of our gorgeous town-house, hoping Mum would show it to everyone I'd grown up with. I'd always wanted to escape. To set out on my own and have adventures, be the kind of person that was too big to be contained in a tiny rural village. I'd wanted more and I'd made no secret of it. "There's no shame in changing your mind, Kaity," she said softly. "Just think about it, okay? If not for you, then for Rex. And for me. Since your dad passed, it's been far too quiet. I'd love to have you here."

"I know you would." I sighed and glanced at the clock. It was past ten now and I still had to figure out what to do about Rex tomorrow. "I have to go, Mum. But you've given me a lot to consider. Thank you."

"I love you."

"I love you, too." I hung up and stared out of the window, listening to the sounds of sirens blazing, foxes screeching, babies crying in the flats up above. It was so tempting to succumb to my mum's talk of village schools and country life. To picture Rex baking with his grandma, playing happily with the cats, running free across empty stretches of golden sand. But I couldn't go backwards. I had to find a way to move forwards. To not be a failure. I had to get to the bottom of the case with Joshua Jones. If I did that, the promotion would be as good as mine and everything would be okay. It *had* to be.

Chapter Nine

Josh

Four months, three weeks and six wonderful days. I couldn't believe I'd actually been seeing Franchesca for so long. By some miracle, she hadn't lost interest in me yet, a fact I was still puzzled by on a daily basis. It had been about a month after our first date when she'd finally brought up the *'what are we?'* elephant in the room, as we'd walked back to her place from a dinner party held by her science boffin friends.

I'd still been reeling from the intense pace of the conversation that had carried on around me all evening, the long words and tedious explanations flying over my head, making me feel ignorant and out of place. Fran's friends were articulate, witty and knowledgable in a way I had never been and *would* never be. We were from different worlds, and it was glaringly obvious that we didn't fit.

She'd been a boarding school child, sent away from home at the age of seven, taught by the finest educators in England, drip fed facts and given the best of everything before she'd even reached puberty. While I was losing my weekly reading book and messing up my list of ten spellings, she had been learning to play the piano, speak French and rising to the top of her classes with a natural proclivity I couldn't even pretend to emulate. She was the same age as me, just twenty-six, and yet she already had her Master's degree and was planning to start her PHD.

I knew that what *I* did was an important job too. But it was in a different league. She was trying to cure cancer. She was changing the world. What I did was so small in comparison. I didn't understand why she would give me the time of day, but whenever I voiced my confusion, she would say it wasn't our differences that mattered. It was our similarities.

Not that our intellectual differences had escaped her attention completely. There were occasions when she couldn't seem to stop herself from teasing me, her eyes wide, her mouth pursed as she held back a laugh when she realised I'd lost track of what she was saying and was struggling to regain my footing. There were times when I saw myself through her eyes and felt like crawling into a hole and curling up into a ball of self pity. I was angry that I had been dealt such different, such vastly inferior cards. That she had experienced so much, and I had been given so little. But it didn't stop me wanting to be around her. I didn't care about the teasing. It didn't matter if she sometimes patted me on the cheek like a stupid but adorable puppy. Nor that she earned almost twice my salary. We were happy. Despite every obstacle, we couldn't deny that we felt something for each other. It shouldn't have worked, but it did.

So when she had asked the question, 'Josh, what *are* we?" I'd gathered my courage and replied, "A couple?" She'd grinned and thrown her arms around me and it had been decided. It still felt too good to be true.

"So, you're off to see the girlfriend tonight then?" Mike's deep voice called, as he came into the work-out room. I pressed the stop button on the treadmill and got off, wiping the sweat from my face with a towel. It had been a long, uneventful shift and we'd all been keeping ourselves busy, reading, working out, playing cards. Some days it felt like we didn't stop, days when we would rush from one call-out to another without pausing for breath. Other times, it was dead. It could be boring, but at least it meant people were safe.

"Yeah," I grinned, tossing the towel on the bench behind me. "I said I'd pick her up from work since her car is in for its MOT." I glanced up at the big, orange faced clock on the wall. It was ten to six, ten minutes until the end of my shift. Franchesca would finish at half past, so I'd have time to pick up dinner and a bottle of wine on my way over to her. I'd have to be quick about it though. I'd made the mistake of being late once and she'd barely spoken to me for a week over it. She had high expectations, and I respected that.

"It's nice to have a woman to go home to after a long day," Mike said, climbing onto the rowing machine, his broad shoulders heaving as he slid back and forth with increasing speed. Mike was the definition of a family man. He'd been with his wife, Lara for twenty-two years, and still claimed it had been love at first sight when a friend of a friend had introduced them at his twentieth birthday party. They had three kids, two boys and a girl and they seemed like the kind of perfect, happy family you only ever see in storybooks. I'd often watched the way Mike interacted with his wife, the casual way they smiled and touched and teased that made marriage look so easy. Fran and I were still so formal, we hadn't yet got to the easy part, but I knew we would.

I took a deep swig from my water bottle and glanced at the clock again. The night shift team should be arriving soon. I wondered if I could slip out a couple of minutes early. I really didn't want to be late. I opened my mouth to ask Mike, just as the deafening tones of the alarm blasted through the station. Mike was off the rowing machine and running to the door in an instant. I felt suddenly nauseous as my legs moved towards the fire engine, knowing I had no choice and yet picturing the expression on Franchesca's face when she realised I wasn't coming for her. There was no time for a call, not even a second to send a text, but she was a smart woman. When I didn't come, she'd realise there had been an emergency. She would understand. I jumped into the driver's seat, flicked on the siren, and put her to the back of my mind. It was all I could do.

The smoke was thick and black, pouring from the open upstairs windows of the smart new-build house in the far corner of the cul-de-sac. The neighbours were gathered outside, shouting over each other in their haste to get to me. As I flung open the door and jumped down onto the pavement, a man grabbed me roughly by the shoulder, spinning me around. My heart flipped in my chest as I saw the terror in his eyes. "My wife and daughters are inside!" he hissed, his fingers tight as they gripped my collar. "They're in there!"

I nodded confidently, though I felt anything but. The bay window downstairs was bright orange with the raging fire, the smell of burning turning the air toxic around us. I looked up and caught sight of the flames licking up the bedroom curtains. "Mike!" I yelled over the gathered crowd. "Three inside!" His face went pale as he followed my gaze to the blazing building. It was always the worst part. Getting the fire under control was difficult enough, the open windows had fed the flames allowing the blaze to rage quickly out of control. But homes could be rebuilt. Possessions replaced. When there were people inside, it changed the game. The stakes became so much higher.

I turned back to the man. "Any idea where they are?"

"They were asleep. In the back bedroom. They've got the flu. Sharon – my wife – she's a deep sleeper at the best of times but she's on the cold and flu meds. What if she's still asleep? What if the kids can't wake her? Shit! I only went out for an hour. The girls are only three. Twins. My baby girls! Please, please get in there. Please, don't let them die! Promise me you won't let them die!"

"Gavin, let the man go! Let him get on with it!" a silver haired neighbour said, yanking him back and keeping a firm hand on his elbow. "You need to stay calm," he insisted. Laurence's authoritative voice boomed over the crowd, ordering them back to the other side of the road. I strode over to Mike and relayed the information. Rebecca had the hose in her hands, steady in her arms as she aimed a powerful jet of water up at the window, yelling instructions over her shoulder as the second engine pulled up, the firefighters jumping out to assist.

"We need to get round the back. Now!" I said. Mike nodded, instructing Brett and Pete to bring the ladder. I rushed ahead, relieved to find the side gate open. Passing the kitchen window, I saw the extent of the fire, the flames roaring mercilessly, the smoke billowing black beneath the ceiling. I guessed it wouldn't be more than a matter of minutes before the whole lot caved in on itself.

Brett leaned the ladder against the wall and Mike clambered up first. I followed close behind. "Window's closed. Cover your head!" Mike yelled. I turned my face toward the ground, my heart thumping in my chest, as the sound of breaking glass rained down around me. Pete tossed up a rubber mat and Mike laid it over the jagged glass on the window frame, clambering inside the building. I raced up the ladder and leaped inside the room. On the mattress beneath a colourful crochet blanket, a blonde haired woman and child were lying unconscious, unaware of the thick noxious grey smoke that was silently suffocating them.

"Where's the other child?" I yelled, glancing around, rushing to the other side of the bed, looking under the bed frame.

Mike threw open the wardrobes. "Not here." He picked up the little girl and rushed to the window, handing her limp body to Brett who was waiting at the top of the ladder. He descended instantly and Mike returned, hitching the woman over his shoulder.

"Captain, I'm going to find her."

Mike's eyes met mine. "Josh," he said, shaking his head. He hesitated, his lips pressed together in a tight line. I knew what he was supposed to say. The warnings he was obligated to give. The fact that it was a lost cause and if she wasn't in this room, she was almost certainly dead. But he was a father. And I knew if it had been his daughter, nothing on earth would make him stop searching when there was still a chance. He paused at the window, the indecision written on his face and I knew I couldn't let him say no. No matter what, I was going anyway. He seemed to read the determination in my expression, and gave a short nod. "You have three minutes," he breathed. "Not a second more." And then he was gone.

I didn't stop to think. I put my gloved hand on the door, wincing at the heat that blasted into the room as I pulled it open. The floor was raging hot beneath my feet and I was hyper aware of the fact that every step could be my last. At any moment, the floor could give way beneath me and I could fall to my death. I didn't allow myself to think of the flames, the heat. All I could think of was the child, alone and in danger in a burning building.

The hall was long and narrow and I could see that the far bedroom, the one at the front, was already a lost cause. The fire had engulfed the stairs and was heading with rapid haste in my direction. My lungs burned, despite the protective mask, my face dripping with sweat, stinging my eyes, my hands shaking as I made my way forward. I darted into a bedroom to the left, searching quickly, tossing aside the single duvet with the Finding Nemo picture on it, looking behind the curtains, almost ripping the wardrobe door from its hinges in my desperation to find the child.

I ran out of the room, back to the hall. Ahead, there was another door, though my heart dropped as I saw how thick the smoke was surrounding it. I rushed towards it, pushing it open, realising it was a bathroom. The smoke was almost blinding, the heat unbearable. I rushed across the room and glanced inside the bathtub, devastated to find it empty. Spinning on my heel, I saw a shower cubicle in the corner of the room. There was a loud crack behind me and I realised with a sense of dread that the floor was seconds from giving way. I had to get out. But not without checking that cubicle first. I could not leave without knowing.

With light footsteps, I made it across the floor and grabbed the handle. The rubber seal had melted and as I swung the cubicle door back, the sticky grey liquid ran in searing streams down the front of my uniform. I felt my throat seize in relief as I saw the tiny figure sprawled on the shower base, her teddy-bear clutched in her unconscious arms. There was no time to check her pulse. I grabbed her in my arms and ran for the door. The flames were licking around the door-frame, paint bubbling and blackening as it boiled beneath the heat of the fire. I put my arm over the little girl's head, running towards the back bedroom. An almighty crash came from behind me and I knew the bathroom floor had caved in. I didn't stop.

I threw open the door, relieved to see Mike's anxious face staring in at the window, and I placed the girl in his arms, clambering out of the window after him. I reached the ground and spun around, seeing Mike running towards the gate, carrying the child to the road where the ambulance had parked a safe distance away. I ripped off my mask, chasing after him. I had to know if she was alright. The waiting crowd erupted into cheers and shouts from the opposite side of the road as I emerged from the gate, my eyes trained on Mike's back, the shouts from the rest of my team as they fought hard against the overpowering flames deafening around me.

"Stand back!" someone yelled suddenly and instinct made me cover my head, turning my body away as the downstairs window exploded, showering glass everywhere.

"Fuck! Gavin!"

I turned to see the man, the little girl's dad, sprawled on his back on the road, his cheek bleeding, his skin dark with soot and sweat. I ran to where he lay, his arms spread wide. "Are you okay?" I said, dropping to my knees beside him.

He blinked and wiped a hand across his cheek, smearing blood and grime over his face. "Is *she?*" he croaked.

I looked up, finding Mike in the crowd. I could just make out the tiny body on the stretcher in the back of the ambulance, an oxygen mask clamped over her little face. Mike gave a nod, putting two thumbs up, a wide smile spread across his face. I looked down at Gavin and nodded. "They're okay. They're alive!"

"Because of *you*. All because of you." He grabbed my collar again and this time there were tears in his eyes. "You're a hero. A bloody hero! Thank you," he sobbed. I looked to the fire ravaged house, and smiled.

Chapter Ten

Josh

It was long past midnight when we finally made it back to the station. Brett traipsed into the kitchen, filling the kettle and flicking the switch, and we all slumped down on the sofas, tired and empty from hours of battling the fire. The house had been in ruins when we'd finally left. There was no way it would be habitable again, it would have to be rebuilt from the ground up. A neighbour had told me that the family had only moved in the year before. They'd lost everything. Their pictures, their books, the children's toys and all their technology. They had nothing. But they'd survived.

We'd already had a report from the hospital. The mother and child who'd been in the bedroom were both off oxygen and breathing unaided. The little girl I'd found in the shower was still in intensive care, intubated and unconscious, but alive. I planned to call again tomorrow to find out how she was doing. I hoped I hadn't been too late. I couldn't bear it if she died now.

Brett placed a cup of tea on the table in front of me and I nodded my thanks. "You know," Mike said, picking up his mug and dipping a chocolate digestive into the milky brew, "Lara won't even have one in the house."

"What?" Rebecca asked, stifling a wide yawn with the back of her hand. She had a long cut running up the back of her forearm from where the window had exploded and she'd shielded her face. The power of the explosion had blasted the glass with such force it had torn through the thick protective material of her bunker gear. As usual, she'd insisted the paramedic deal with it at the scene so she didn't have to leave us short-handed. I'd heard her yelling it was only a scratch, allowing the paramedic to spray it with antiseptic before running back to the blazing building. I was proud of her. Of all of us.

"An iron," Mike continued. "Says it's not worth the risk. I always tell her it's because she can't stand the thought of doing my shirts, but after what we just saw, I'll take the dry cleaners any day."

"I can't believe he went out and left it switched on, sitting on the table right next to a newspaper!" Brett said, shaking his head. "Right beside the bloody alcohol cabinet too. People just don't think."

"I don't think he'll make the same mistake again," I said. Gavin had been horrified when he realised he was the one who had started the fire. He'd done a pile of ironing to help out his wife since she was ill with the flu, and then nipped out to the supermarket to pick up the weekly shop. He'd meant to help, to make life easier, and yet, his inattention to detail had nearly killed them all.

"You did well tonight," Mike said, looking at me now. "That took some serious guts to go looking for the girl."

"It's my job," I said simply. "You'd have done the same."

He gave a tiny imperceptible nod. It was true, he would have done. He and I were cut from the same cloth. I was lucky to have him leading the team – a lot of captains wouldn't have let me take such a risk. I'd have lost my job for going against orders, because in a case like that, I would have *had* to break the rules. I was grateful Mike hadn't pushed me to make that choice.

"Well," Brett said, standing up and stretching his arms high above him. He gave a loud yawn and grinned. "It's Friday night and we're officially off duty. Who fancies a few drinks before bed?"

"Not me," Mike said, getting to his feet. "I have a warm woman and a soft bed waiting for me, and that's exactly where I'm heading. Night all. And well done for today. I'm proud of you." He picked up his jacket and left the kitchen. I heard him go downstairs, handing over to the night team.

"Josh?" Brett said, flashing a wink my way. "How about it?"

I shook my head, suddenly aware that I hadn't checked my phone. A cold feeling of dread spread through my stomach and I coughed as my tea hit the back of my throat. I hadn't had a moment to think about Franchesca since the alarm had gone off all those hours before. There had been a chance it could have been a cat stuck up a tree or a baby locked in a car. A quick job that would have had me back in time to spend the evening with her, all-be-it a little late. The nature of this job was that you never knew what it was you were heading in to. You had to be ready for the worst possible scenario and that was exactly what had happened tonight.

Brett made a quip about being under the thumb and turned his attention to Pete and Laurence. I reached across to the coat hooks and pulled my phone from my jacket. My heart sank as I saw the screen. Fifty-four missed calls, seventeen voice-mails and five texts. Surely she would have realised what had happened? I slipped out of the kitchen, making my way down the hall into the empty TV room, holding my phone to my ear. I hoped she was okay. That she hadn't been in her own emergency whilst I'd been off dealing with the fire.

The clipped tones of the automated message announced the first voicemail.

"Message left at six twenty-nine p.m."

"Josh, I'm outside in the bus shelter. Are you here?"

"Message left at six thirty-two p.m."

"If you're going to be late, let me know. I've had a long day."

"Message left at six thirty-five p.m."

"Josh, you could at least send a text. Are you coming or not?"

"Message left at six forty three p.m."

"Where the fuck are you? Do you think I want to be waiting outside for you like a fucking loser? Get here now!"

"Message left at six fifty p.m."

"Don't fucking bother coming. I've called a taxi. Thanks a lot for wasting my time! I can't believe I actually thought you were a gentleman. You're a joke, Josh. A fucking joke."

There were a further twelve voice-mails, each more angry and accusing, asking if I was out with another girl, if I had forgotten her, why I didn't value her time, why I had no manners. That stung worse than the rest. Manners were one of the few things I did have going for me. I put the phone on the table and realised my hands were shaking. How could she be so angry? So mean? It wasn't fair.

"Josh? You okay?" I looked up. Rebecca was standing in the doorway, frowning. "You need a strong drink or something?"

I shook my head. "I'm okay. Thank you. Just a long day, that's all. Just tired."

She nodded. "You and me both. I'm heading off now. See you in a few days, okay?"

"Yeah."

"Seriously, get some rest, Josh." She looked at me with concern and I tried to form my face into some impression of a smile.

"I will. See you next week."

I watched her go and turned back to my phone. It was one thirty in the morning and I had no idea what Franchesca would want me to do. Should I call her? Go round to her place? I couldn't decide if she'd be more angry if I woke her up now, or would it be worse if I did nothing? It was so confusing. After the day I'd had, I just wanted to cuddle up to her and sleep for a really long time. Maybe she'd calmed down now, realised her mistake. She'd been tired and fed up and not considered the simplest explanation for my absence. I decided on a text.

Hi Franchesca, I'm so sorry I wasn't there to pick you up from work. A last minute emergency came up and I've only just got back to the station. I'm sorry there was no time to text. I hope you weren't worried. It's late, so I'll let you sleep and give you a call in the morning. Josh. X

I read it three times and then with a sigh, I pressed send, hoping I was doing the right thing.

Chapter Eleven

Josh

The phone rang and rang and with a sigh, I heard the click as it cut to Franchesca's voicemail again. I didn't leave a message. I was terrible with voicemail at the best of times, always fumbling my words and messing up what I meant to say. I'd slept heavily after the exertions of the evening, dreaming of flames and smoke and screams that never stopped. When I finally woke, with the mid-morning sun casting its buttery glow around my bedroom, I realised I felt more tired than I had before I went to bed.

I nursed my coffee now, typing and deleting texts before I could send them. I hated the uncertainty of the situation, knowing she was upset with me and not knowing how to fix it. If she would only tell me, I would do it in an instant. It was the guessing that made me tense up.

I picked up my phone again, this time ignoring Franchesca's number and keying in the digits for the hospital. The call was answered on the second ring and I asked to be transferred to the children's ward, hoping they wouldn't be pedantic about giving me an update. I scratched my chin, the dark stubble rough against my fingers. I needed a good shave and a long shower after this, I decided. Clear my head.

The line crackled and a woman's voice answered. "Sister speaking, how may I help?"

"Oh, hi, yeah, I'm calling about the twins who were brought in yesterday? Two little girls, three years old. They were in a house fire."

"Name?"

"Ruby and Bethany Payton," I said, reading off the paper I'd scribbled their details on.

"No, your name, I mean."

"Oh, Joshua. Joshua Jones. I'm one of the firefighters who got them out."

"So, you're not related to them?"

"No, but I was told that if I called, I would be updated on their recovery."

"I'm sorry, Mr. Jones, I – hold on a minute."

There was a pause and I heard voices speaking quickly, though I couldn't make out what they were saying. The Sister came back on the line. "It's your lucky day, Mr. Jones. Their father is here. He wants to speak to you."

I smiled in relief, glad I wouldn't be left wondering. I couldn't stop thinking about them, their tiny faces covered with oxygen masks. I couldn't imagine what Gavin must be feeling right now.

"Josh, I'm so glad you called," Gavin's voice came over the line. "I was going to ring the station to thank you again, but I haven't had chance."

"Of course not, I doubt you've had much sleep," I said. "How are they?"

I heard a deep sigh and held my breath, waiting for the worst. "They're okay. All of them. Sharon is awake and breathing on her own, though she's got a hell of a nasty cough. Ruby's a bit peaky too but she's had a bite to eat and she's sitting up now. She's already complaining about not being allowed to go in the playroom yet. They've said she needs to wait until tomorrow."

"And... and Bethany?" I asked, picturing her limp body as I'd hauled her from the shower cubicle, the sound of the floor that had given way just seconds later.

His voice cracked. "She's awake. And they removed the intubator thingy earlier this morning. She can't remember a thing. It's likely she passed out and hit her head on the way down, though there's no obvious wound, so *that's* something. The doctor said she was very lucky to be alive, and that the seal of the shower cubicle must have kept the worst of the smoke out. I can't believe they're all okay. I thought I'd lost them. I really did. It makes me sick to my stomach to think where I would be right now if it weren't for you."

"There's really no need to thank me," I replied, swallowing back a lump in my throat. "I was just doing my job."

"Your job saved their lives. And mine." There was a short pause and I heard him sniff. "Anyway, I have to go, I told Ruby I'd bring her some magazines to keep her occupied."

"You do that. And thanks for the update," I grinned. "I'm so glad they're all okay. And I'm sorry about your home."

"Doesn't matter. When you come that close to losing everyone you love, everything else loses its value. We can start again. We still have each other."

Gavin hung up and I nodded to myself. He was right. The thing that mattered was the love between people, not the little disagreements and silly misunderstandings. I couldn't let Fran spend the day brooding, and risk her walking away from what we had, over something so small as me not picking her up from work. I pushed my coffee away and stood up, heading for the shower. If she wouldn't answer my calls, I'd just have to go round to her house. I wouldn't give up without a fight.

Chapter Twelve

Josh

I wiped the rain from my eyes, blinking up at the bedroom window where I'd seen Franchesca's furious face peering down at me several minutes previously. Either she was taking her time coming to let me in, or she'd decided to make me stand out in the rain until I gave up and left. The summer storm had appeared out of nowhere, the dark grey clouds masking the piercing blue sky I'd woken up to earlier.

I banged on the door again, frustration spreading through me, then pulled my leather jacket tighter around my body, my legs itching beneath the sodden denim of my jeans. There was a sense of injustice to the whole awful situation. It wasn't as if I'd stood her up on purpose. I'd *wanted* to be there to collect her. But my job wasn't exactly the kind you could postpone. If I had even paused to send a text, I'd have lost crucial seconds and that trapped little girl would have died. It wasn't fair for Fran to treat me so badly when I'd done the only thing I could do.

I raised my fist to knock again and the door swung open. Franchesca stood there dressed in a sheer cream satin nightgown, an expectant look on her face.

"Fran."

"Well, come in then," she said, as if it had been me keeping her waiting all along. I stepped inside, shaking the rain from my jacket. She pushed the door closed and turned, staring up at me. Now that I was here I didn't know what to say. "Look, Franchesca. I'm sorry I didn't call. I would have been there as we planned, but – "

"Stop." A frown puckered her forehead and she held up a hand to my face. "I don't want to talk about it."

"But – "

"No, Josh." She shook her head.

"So, you're not angry?" I asked, feeling more confused than ever.

"I didn't say that, did I?" She pursed her lips and I saw the unmistakable flash of fury in her eyes. She breathed in, her nostrils flaring and then, with what looked like considerable effort, she smiled. "I think it's best if we put this... incident, in a locked box and throw away the key. Don't you?"

I shrugged. It sounded to me like the complete opposite of what we should do, especially as I was afraid of how she might react if the same thing happened again – and it *would* happen again. It was bound to. But conflict, especially when it came to women, was not my strong suit, and here she was offering me an easy way out. I nodded slowly. "If you're sure?"

She smiled, the warmth returning to her eyes and I felt the cold feeling I'd been carrying round in my stomach since last night evaporate. She looked coyly down, her fingertips moving to slip the thin strap of her nightdress over the curve of her tanned shoulder. The silky material slid down the length of her body, pooling at her ankles. "I know how you can make it up to me," she said, her voice as smooth as honey as she stepped forward. "You *do* want to, don't you Josh?"

Chapter Thirteen

Josh

Eleven Months Later

"What do you mean, they want to honour you?"

I clasped the thick cream envelope in both hands, bowing my head towards the polished wooden floorboards, cringing at the familiar cool tone which I knew meant trouble. I'd put off telling Franchesca the news for as long as I possibly could, hoping there had been a mistake, or that perhaps the whole thing would just get cancelled.

When Mike had told me that he'd put me forward for the Queen's Gallantry Medal for bravery, I'd felt so proud and humbled I'd had to leave the room I was so overcome with emotion. The award was the kind of honour that came once in a lifetime, if at all. An absolute highpoint in any fire-fighter's career, to be awarded by the Queen herself. Even being nominated meant the world to me. It made my chest physically hurt with pride to know that Mike and the rest of my team recognised the lengths I was prepared to go to in the course of my work.

But I knew Fran wouldn't see it that way. When she'd told me that she didn't want to talk about it almost a year ago, I hadn't realised she meant *ever*. It had been near impossible to avoid the subject at the time. My face had been plastered over the front pages of both the local and national newspapers. Everywhere we went, people would stop me to shake my hand or slap me on the back with tears in their eyes. It should have been the best time of my life. But instead, I'd squashed down my pride and done everything I could to divert the attention away from myself. I'd turned down opportunities for radio interviews and even TV appearances, much to the disgust of Brett and Mike. They couldn't understand that it was just easier not to go. They didn't realise that for me, Fran came first. She *had* to. But this award was awkward in a way nothing else had come close to. You didn't just refuse an honour like this. And if I was being honest with myself, I didn't want to.

"I would have told you sooner," I said gently,

placing the envelope on the kitchen table and offering an apologetic smile. "Only, I didn't know for sure if it was just speculation. There's going to be a ceremony. At Buckingham Palace... it's quite a big deal."

Franchesca placed her wine glass down on the draining board and turned, leaning against the sink, her arms folded as she met my eyes from across the room. Hers were hard and cold, her lips pressed so tightly together they were blanched white. I hated when she was like this. It made me anxious. Since I'd given up my flat and moved in with her six months previously, I'd found there were more and more things added to the list of 'Franchesca's triggers.' I couldn't blame her for being stuck in her ways – she'd lived alone for a long time before I'd invaded her space, but still, it had come as a hell of a surprise to discover just how easy she was to provoke. Not that I ever intended to.

"Tell them no," she said, her eyes not leaving mine. Her tone was offhand, but I knew she meant it.

"Fran, I can't."

"Of course you can." She strode across to the

table, picking the letter up, tearing the envelope as she pulled the crisp white invitation from it. She jabbed her finger at it. "You call this number and you tell them you're declining the award. It's not fucking rocket science, Joshua."

I sighed. "This is a big deal. A medal from the *Queen*, Franchesca. It's not the kind of thing that comes round often. It shines a light on my whole team, not just me. Mike, Brett – " I stopped myself from mentioning Rebecca's name. I didn't need yet another repeat of that reoccurring argument right now. Fran hated that there was a woman on the team and had called Rebecca just about every name under the sun since the moment they met. I was prepared to let a lot go when it came to my girlfriend, but I could never stand for her to be cruel about Rebecca. She was a brave, hard working woman, a good friend and the fact that I wouldn't hear meanness and spite about her made Fran all the more furious. It was just another thing to add to the list.

I sighed and stepped closer to her. "We're all part of this. If I refuse, they'll miss out too. It wouldn't be right."

"So? Why should I care?" She walked casually back to the sink, though I could see the tension in her shoulders. I watched silently as she refilled her wine glass and took a sip. She didn't offer me a glass.

I stepped forward again. "You're invited too. It's not like I'll be going without you. You can wear that blue dress that you got for the Healthcare Science Award ceremony. She spun around and I knew instantly that I'd said the wrong thing. I gripped the edge of the counter, biting hard at the inside of my cheek, wishing I could swallow my words.

"Oh really, how nice!" she simpered sarcastically. "Because the only thing more fun than being humiliated at *my* award ceremony in front of my peers, would be to stand up and clap while you get people falling over themselves to tell you just how magnificent you are. Is that right?"

"You weren't humiliated. You were nominated and you came second. Where's the humiliation in that? There's nothing to be ashamed of. This isn't me trying to one up you. This is completely different," I said, struggling to find the right words.

"Don't you dare tell me it's not the same! How dare you even ask it of me when you know what I just went through. I deserved that award. I worked hard for it and if Peter McGuinness hadn't been lining the judges' pockets, it would have been me standing up there picking up first place."

"I know. I know, and I'm sorry you didn't win. And nobody knows how hard you work more than me. But you'll get another opportunity next year. I might never get this chance again. Don't you see how crazy it is to keep going with this silly grudge, just because I stood you up one time? I was doing my job, for gods sake! Saving those little girls lives. *I* don't even understand it – how on earth am I supposed to explain it to my workmates? They'll think I've lost the plot. Please, Fran, can't we just move on from that ridiculous argument and you be happy for me. Can't you just be happy for me?"

She stared at me, her eyes fixed on my face, her hands visibly shaking as she gripped the wine glass. For a moment I wondered if I'd broken through the storm. If for once in all our time together, she might actually be considering my point of view. Then, she screwed up her face into a mask of pure fury and hurled her wine glass straight at my head. I felt the impact as it collided with my cheekbone, the smell of rich Merlot, the sharp sting as the glass shattered against my face, tearing through my skin. A second later, I felt the warm trickle of blood, tasted it on my lips.

"You aren't going," she whispered, her voice trembling on the words. She picked up the wine bottle by the neck and stormed out of the kitchen, slamming the door behind her.

Chapter Fourteen

Josh

The sound of laughter broke through my consciousness and I looked across the table to find Brett and Mike in an animated discussion over what they were planning to wear to the award ceremony at Buckingham Palace next week. The ceremony itself would be a very serious affair, with recipients of various medals lining up to be given them personally by the Queen, and only Mike and Brett had been invited to join me from the station. However, a huge party had been organised for after the ceremony and the whole team was intending to come to mark the occasion. I couldn't be sure how long I'd zoned out for, my constant worry over upsetting Franchesca and how I could get her to see my point of view running on a loop through my mind.

I hadn't slept properly in the three nights since we'd argued, sick with worry about the whole situation. The cut on my cheek wasn't a deep one, and after a quick wipe with a damp cloth, the bleeding had stopped, but every mirror I passed reminded me of what she had done. How out of control she had seemed in the heat of the moment.

When I'd felt the hot sting of my skin splitting open, the bruise blooming deep beneath the surface, I'd been taken right back to my childhood. I'd felt like the scared little boy who used to wet his pants at the sound of disapproval in his mother's voice, all my confidence evaporating in an instant.

Was *this* what it meant to be with a woman? Did all men give in to their partner's demands or suffer the consequences if not? I looked at Mike and Brett now, their easy confidence, their self-assured presence and couldn't imagine either of them bowing down to anyone. Mike was a gentleman, a good man, but he wasn't a pushover. And Lara, his wife, seemed to respect him for that. Of course they argued. They had disagreements. But neither one of them expected total obedience. And I would have bet anything that Lara had never smashed a wine glass into Mike's face.

"I'm telling you, it's pure muscle," Brett exclaimed, flexing his biceps comically. "It's no surprise I need to go up a size – "

"Or three!" Mike cut in. Brett raised an eyebrow and continued unflustered. "When you're this ripped, it's not easy finding the perfect suit." He glanced over to me. "No doubt Joshua here has just the same issue."

"Ha! Except Josh is pure muscle. You're mostly meat and spud pie," Mike teased. "Josh, you hiring or buying?" he called down the table, still grinning as Brett attempted to make his pecs dance.

"Huh?"

"Your suit. For the ceremony?"

"Oh..." I took a deep breath. "I'm not sure. I actually don't know if I can make it. Franchesca has... her grandmother is coming to stay that weekend," I improvised, knowing how ridiculous my paltry excuse sounded.

Brett and Mike looked at me, their grins disappearing simultaneously. "What do you mean, you're not going to come?" Brett asked, shaking his head slowly. "This is *your* big day. It's *your* award. You *have to* be there!"

"I know that, but..."

"But nothing," Mike said. "This is an honour. A privilege. And you want to show us up because you've got a house guest? What's the matter with you?" Mike said, all the warmth gone from his tone.

"I don't want to upset Fran."

"Why should she be upset? Surely she's proud of you?"

"I – "

"And unless you want to let down the whole team, you're damn well going to be there! This is a big deal for all of us, Josh. We want to see one of our own recognised for the work we do. I can't believe you'd even consider not turning up."

Brett pushed back his chair and walked round the large wooden table, coming to perch on the scratched surface beside me. I found I couldn't seem to look him in the eye. "What's this really about, mate? What's going on?"

I shook my head. "I just don't want to upset anyone."

"And that's what makes you such a fucking

diamond, mate. You're selfless. It's why you didn't think twice about going in after little Bethany. Why she's playing hopscotch and dolls with her twin rather than rotting in a coffin. It's why you would do it all again in a heartbeat and why you're being given a fucking medal from Her Majesty herself. Because you deserve it."

"Yes, you bloody do," Mike said. "So if this is your attempt at being humble, stop it. Stand up and be proud."

Brett clapped me on the shoulder and I raised my head to look at him. "Forget about us. Forget about Fran's granny and your overdeveloped sense of humility. What do *you* want to do?"

I stared at him. "I want to go."

"Good. Then you're going." Brett grinned and looked at Mike. "I bet this bastard is going to try and outshine me in his suit."

"He wouldn't have to try hard," Mike grinned.

Chapter Fifteen

Josh

Four times I tried to bring up the subject of the award ceremony with Franchesca. I wanted her there with me. I wanted to feel the eyes on us as we walked in together and think 'yes!' she chose *me*. She's with *me*. I couldn't shake the feeling that this should have been one of the happiest occasions of my life, and yet I was wishing it away so I didn't have to worry about it anymore.

Every time I even got close to bringing it up, I would see the hardness return to her face, the stubborn resolve. In the end, I decided to take the easy way out. I told her I was on duty, though I had the day off, and collected my suit from the swanky hire shop, taking it straight to the fire-station with me to get ready.

Brett came into the changing rooms just as I was stepping out of the shower. "So, you're flying solo tonight?" he asked, stripping out of his clothes with a level of confidence I could only dream of. I secured my towel tighter around my waist as he stepped under the stream of the shower, turning the temperature up to hot.

The steam billowed around us as I nodded. "Yeah, you know. Fran's got her auntie staying."

"I thought you said it was her grandma?"

"Did I? Hmm. It's her great aunt."

"Maybe I'll swing by yours tomorrow. Give her some of the old Brett Sinclair charm. Old girls love me."

I made a non-committal noise, wondering how I was going to talk him out of that. I could just picture Franchesca's face when she realised I'd been telling lies to my workmates. But then, what was I supposed to tell them? The *truth?*

"What about you," I asked, keen to change the subject. "Is Millie your plus one tonight?"

"Yeah, she's coming." He stepped out of the shower and I turned away, pulling the crisp white shirt from its hanger and slipping my arms into it. "Actually, mate, it's going pretty well."

"It's the longest I can ever remember you sticking

with one woman," I replied, buttoning the shirt.

"Yeah... I think this could be it."

"It?"

"The one."

I turned, catching the unfamiliar sight of a blush on his cheeks before he covered his face with his towel. "Wow," I breathed. "I never thought I'd see the day Brett Sinclair was actually in love. Good for you, mate," I grinned. "Brett Sinclair, tamed by a woman!"

"Shut up!" He threw the towel at me and I ducked.

"Put some bloody underwear on," I laughed, shielding my eyes. "We're going to be late!"

I slid the key in the lock, stumbling as I tried to balance the velvet covered medal box in one hand, squinting as I turned the key one way and then another. It was gone two a.m. and I hoped that Franchesca would be sound asleep by now. I knew she'd be livid when she realised where I'd been.

The door remained firmly closed and I jiggled the handle, my vision blurring. I definitely should have said no to that last pint, but for once in my life, I'd been having too much fun to consider the consequences. Without warning, the front door swung open and I squinted, trying to figure out what was wrong with the picture in front of me.

Fran was standing there, her hair artfully curled, her make-up perfect, her nightdress brushing against her bare knees. I had a sudden flashback to the time I'd arrived at her house to grovel for forgiveness in the pouring rain, the way she'd surprised me by inviting me in, taking me to bed. I glanced down at her face and realised what was so out of place in the situation. Fran was smiling. Not just smiling, but looking at me with hunger. Lust. Perhaps all along, all this time, she'd been waiting for me to stand up to her.

I'd heard time and time again, nice guys finish last, bad boys get the girl. It hadn't been my intention, but if *this* was the consequence of standing my ground, maybe I'd have to try it more often.

"So," she said with a sideways smile. "The hero returns."

"I – I'm..." I stuttered.

She turned and walked towards the living room. I watched her disappear through the door, feeling suddenly stone cold sober. I stepped inside, pushing the front door closed behind me and with a sense of mingled excitement and dread, I followed after her.

All sense of worry left my body the moment I saw the room. Franchesca had lit dozens of candles, placing them on every flat surface, a soft glow illuminating her in the middle of the room. She'd thrown down the big floor cushions on the carpet, creating a makeshift bed, and I felt my face break into a wide smile as I saw her sprawled across them, her nightdress riding up so I could see the lace of her underwear.

"A returning hero deserves a hero's welcome. I'm sure you'd agree?" She held out a hand towards me and I swallowed, letting her pull me down onto the floor bed. I moved to roll her onto her back, but she put a hand to my chest, shaking her head. Without a word, she stripped off my suit jacket, my shirt, my smart navy trousers and finally my boxers, before shoving me onto my back. She flashed me a grin before climbing on top of me.

I was in heaven. This was the perfect end to a brilliant evening. This woman would never stop surprising me and that was what I loved about her. I arched up, trying to pull her closer and she slapped my hands away. "Uh uh, no touching. I have a treat for you." She picked up a pillar candle from the coffee table and grinned.

"Fran, what – ahhh," I breathed as she tipped it, dripping the hot wax across my chest. The pain mixed with pleasure was surprisingly enjoyable, though not something I'd ever thought to try before. I'd never seen her like this. I realised I liked it.

"Oh, you like a bit of pain, do you?" She put the candle down, her hips never stopping as they swerved and bucked against me. My head swam and I leaned back against the cushions, sensation overtaking me. There was a loud crack and my eyes shot open as I felt the hot sting of her palm ricochet against my cheek.

"Fran!"

"What?" she asked, her voice sweet and teasing. "Don't you like it? I know you do."

She was right. The sting of her slap heightened my senses, made every sensation stronger. I grinned, feeling my face redden. This was new and exciting, but I'd never been the type for talking in the bedroom. It wasn't my style. Fran didn't need me to speak though. She slapped me again and I groaned, my breath coming harder as I let my eyes sink closed, waiting impatiently for the next little dose of pain.

I opened my eyes, looking up at her flushed face. Her fist collided hard with my mouth. Blood splattered instantly, confusion rushing through me. I tried to speak and choked on a mouthful of the metallic liquid. Fran was still moving, her hips taking me deeper into her body, but her face was hard and cruel as she looked down on me. She raised her fist and punched me again, the full force of it meeting my eye-socket.

"Fran! What the hell!" I yelled, turning my face away, spitting blood onto the cushion. I tried to lift her off of me but she leaned down, clamping her fingernails into my shoulders, digging and ripping deep into my skin. "Franchesca! Stop! Stop this!" I yelled, feeling panicked now.

"Don't tell me this is too much for you?" she said through gritted teeth. "Don't tell me a hero like you can't take a little play fighting?" She punched me again, this one landing on my temple. Black spots showered my vision and I blinked them away. I felt like I was in a nightmare. A prank gone horribly wrong. What was she doing? Why would my own girlfriend be so sick as to seduce me and then do *this?* I couldn't make sense of it. She stiffened and cried out and I stared in shocked silence as she threw her head back. She gave a little sigh of pleasure, the same sigh I'd always listened for and loved, then she leaned forward with a cold, venomous smile.

Without missing a beat, she clambered off me, getting to her feet and with a look of absolute hatred, she stamped her heel into the tender space just beneath my ribs. "Welcome home, hero," she spat. She walked out of the room and I heard her measured footsteps as she climbed the stairs to our bedroom. I rolled onto my side, pulling my knees to my chest and for the first time since I was a little boy, I cried.

Chapter Sixteen

Josh

Dawn was only just breaking over the horizon as I pulled on my trainers and left the house. I hadn't dared to go up to the bedroom to put on my running gear, but I'd found a pair of shorts and a sweaty t-shirt screwed up in my gym bag in the cupboard under the stairs and pulled them on, grateful not to have to go jogging in my suit. Not that I'd ever be able to return *that*. After I'd finally climbed out of the fetal position last night, I'd realised just how far my blood had splattered. The jacket was stained in several patches and I knew I wouldn't be able to summon the courage to take it to the cleaners. I couldn't bear the thought of being asked how it had happened.

The morning air was cold, burning my lungs as I sprinted towards the park, making my eyes water even more. My lip was swollen beyond recognition, and my left eye had sealed itself firmly shut, a deep purple bruise spread wide over the surface of my skin. For a while, lying there on the living room carpet, listening to Franchesca roll and turn in the bedroom above, I'd been able to convince myself it hadn't been that bad. That I was just drunk and over-sensitive. It was just new, this bondage thing, or whatever it was they called it.

But when the sounds of movement overhead ceased and I finally got up to look in the mirror, there had been no denying what she'd done. My whole face had been covered in dried blood, it was in my hair, splattered across my neck, matting my eyelashes in clumps – it was everywhere. When I'd washed the worst off at the kitchen sink, the sight of my face had been no less shocking. This wasn't the result of a little sexual fantasy taken a bit far. This was a fucking mess. She'd *meant* to hurt me. The look in her eyes had been pure hatred. This was my punishment for breaking her rules.

I ran across the road, heading through the gates of the park, hoping it was early enough that I wouldn't see anyone I knew. It was a relief to be outside, out of the house, out of her grasp. It was ridiculous to admit, even to myself, but she frightened me. No. More than that. She made me feel weak and helpless in a way no woman had since my mother. She wasn't the woman I thought she was.

There had been warnings. I knew that now. It was so painfully obvious. But I'd ignored them because I loved her. Because I knew how hard it was to find someone who wanted you, not just for a night, or two, but for the long run. Life before Franchesca had been lonely and monotonous and because of that, I'd accepted her flaws, willing to put up with them if it meant I got the good bits too. But she'd gone too far, even for me. I knew what I had to do. There was no choice to be made, I had to leave. To end it. Because if I didn't, this *would* happen again. I could see now who she was and what she was capable of. And I would rather be alone than live that life again.

It hurt to realise that our relationship, the first real relationship I'd ever had, was at an end. That I'd never get to hold her hand or hear her laugh again. I would wake up every morning from now on, alone in the silence of some empty, soulless flat. I would have to find somewhere new, of course. I'd given up my flat when I'd moved in with Franchesca, only too happy to leave it for what I hoped was something better. But now, I wished I'd kept it. If I had, I'd have somewhere to go now, a place that was safe and out of her reach. Where she couldn't get to me.

I shuddered and realised I was dangerously close to crying again. How was it possible to be so afraid of such a small woman? I could only imagine how Brett would react if he could see me now. He would ask why I hadn't thrown her off me and put her in her place? Why hadn't I just grabbed her by the wrists and told her to stop?

I stopped running, my side aching where she'd kicked me. I couldn't seem to catch my breath. I lowered myself gingerly onto a bench facing out towards the grassy expanse of the park, and let my head drop to my hands. *Of course* Brett wouldn't understand. Nobody would. It was hard for *me* to even make sense of it. But more than any other lesson I'd been taught as a boy, the biggest had been that a man must *never* lay a finger on a woman. No matter what. It was why, even as I overtook my mother in height and weight, she could still make me cower at the slightest hitch in her tone, the merest raise of an eyebrow.

There were a few times, long before I'd learned the fruitlessness of fighting back, when I'd tried to stand up for myself. I let my mind wander to the bleak memories of my childhood now. I'd been five when I'd committed the ultimate sin in my mother's eyes. I'd forgotten to take off my shoes when I came in from playing outside. She'd had a guest that day, a lady called Barbara who lived in the tower-block round the corner and who always smelled of cat wee. I'd known as soon as I ran into the living room by the way Mum caught my eye, that I'd made some kind of mistake, but I'd been so frozen with fear, unsure what exactly it was, that I hadn't thought to look at my feet. It could have been any of a thousand things, but stupid with my own terror, I hadn't thought of the shoes.

I'd crouched down, ignoring the blazing heat from the roaring open fire, sitting in silence, my back poker straight against the wall, my legs crossed tightly as I listened to Mum and Barbara say horrible things about their mutual friends. Mum refused to even look at me. Hours passed in the suffocating heat, and I longed to crack open a window or get a drink of water, but I didn't dare. I knew I shouldn't move. She didn't even have to say a word. I just knew.

Finally, Barbara got up, telling me how lovely it was to see a young boy who didn't think the world revolved around him, praising my mother for my silence. And then she left, Mum walking her to the front door. Still, I didn't move. There had been a long, horrible silence – she liked to make me wait. Sometimes the suspense and anticipation grew too frightening for me and I would wet my pants. I got the feeling she liked that. It gave her more reason to punish me. Pushed her right over the edge, and made her feel all the more justified in her actions. Her *teachings,* she called it. Her footsteps came slowly from the front door, and she stepped inside the room, glaring at me. I didn't speak. Didn't even breathe.

There was a long moment where neither of us moved, and then, just as I knew she would, she launched herself at me, her open hand slapping me hard across one cheek, then the other. She grabbed my feet yanking hard at the lace up shoes, twisting my ankles painfully as she prized them from my feet. She threw them hard at my head and I didn't dare to put my arms up to defend my face. It would only make her more angry. "You filthy little cretin! Coming into my house, wearing your disgusting muddy shoes all over my pristine carpet and then keeping them on the whole of Mrs. Crosby's visit! I ought to whip you senseless!"

She turned, and I felt my stomach drop as I saw where her eyes had been drawn. I didn't have many toys. In fact, I knew exactly how many I *did* have. Three. A half deflated football I'd won in a match from a boy at school. An old spinning top that I'd found in the loft. And *him*. My Fireman Sam action figure. *He* wasn't old or found. He was brand new.

Mum didn't believe in giving presents for no reason. I'd never had birthday gifts or Christmas stockings. But the day we'd gone into town to pick up a parcel she'd missed at the post office, she'd been in the best kind of mood. I'd remembered to open every door for her, I'd complimented her hair do and her dress and she'd been unusually smily. It was a rare, good day and I wasn't going to do anything to spoil it.

The post office was located in a weird, haberdashery shop. Overcrowded shelves spilled over with baskets filled with colourful wool, assorted crayons, crepe paper and picture books. Right at my eye level, cleverly placed, was a shelf filled with toys. Usually, there were a few dolls there, maybe a wooden train set, or in summer, buckets and spades. I always tried not to look at them. Mum would have considered it rude of me. *Begging with my eyes,* she called it. But that day, along with the usual collection of ordinary toys, *he* was there.

I'd seen the cartoon, only when Mum went out and left me alone, of course. I'd read the storybooks over the shoulders of my school friends. And I'd watched the real life firemen arrive like heroes to our crowded, run down estate, and save the day time and time again. I hadn't realised there could be toys of cartoon characters. As I tried to drag my gaze away from him now, I knew with absolute certainty that I had never wanted anything more.

"Oh, look, Joshua. It's one of those firemen toys. I don't suppose you've seen the cartoon, have you?" Mum said, turning to smile at the woman at the counter. "My boy isn't one to waste his time with television." I bowed my head silently, feeling my cheeks redden, hoping this wasn't about to become one of her tests. *Did she know my secret?*

"Oh, my little nephew *loves* Fireman Sam," the woman smiled. "He has one of these figures and plays with it all the time. Young boys do love to play the hero, don't they?" she smiled. "This one is on sale, if you're interested?" she said, flashing me a wink. I looked down at the ground again, wishing we could leave. I knew better than to hope for something so big.

"Well..." Mum said slowly. "Oh, why not? You deserve a treat, Joshua. You've been on fine form today." I couldn't believe what was happening as she lifted the action figure from the shelf and held it out towards me.

"I – oh, thank you... thank you so much, that is so kind of you," I said, repeating the phrases I knew she would want me to say. It wasn't hard, not with a gift like this. I could hardly get my words out in my excitement. Not only was my mother giving me a present for the first time in my life, but it was the thing I would have wanted above all other toys, if only I'd known of its existence. It was the most precious thing I'd ever owned. I'd felt ready to burst with pride and happiness that day, and as the weeks passed and she didn't take the toy from me, I began to relax. To hope it really was mine to keep.

In the end, though, I'd ruined it all, just because I'd forgotten to take off my shoes. How could I have been so stupid? I could feel the beginnings of a lump forming on my forehead from the impact of the shoe. I watched in horror as she picked up my most treasured toy from the shelf. I was too well trained to leave it lying around. I always put it back, tidily on the bookshelf when I wasn't playing with it. Even if I was just popping to the toilet, I knew better than to leave it strewn on the carpet. Now, I wished I'd thought to hide it somewhere safe.

"You don't deserve this," Mum said, breathing hard. "You humiliated me in front of my friend, you disrespected my house and you do not deserve treats."

I seemed to move without realising it, my desperation to save my prized possession overtaking every other instinct. Mum's mouth dropped open as I rushed towards her, arms outstretched as if I could save him. I made a grab for him, and in my haste, missed and pushed her instead, my palms colliding with her stomach. She stumbled back, shocked, then regained her footing.

With an expression of pure malice, she ripped the head off the doll, throwing it into the roaring open fire. I watched in horror as it bubbled and melted, the acrid smell of smouldering plastic filling the room, Fireman Sam's face distorting, blackening. She tossed the headless body to the ground and grabbed me by the collar. "You're going to regret that, Joshua. I'm going to make you wish you'd never been born."

***

I opened my eyes now, almost surprised to find myself sitting on a park bench, my mother long gone, having died of a heart-attack nine years previously, and an entirely new woman causing me anxiety and fear. The weeks that had followed the Fireman Sam incident had been horrific. They'd taught me, above anything, that to fight was pointless. That to raise a hand against a woman, even to defend something important, was an invitation to more pain. I would never be able to restrain Franchesca. I'd had that instinct beaten out of me until it no longer existed. So my only choice was to leave.

"Josh?"

I looked up in surprise, my body curling in on itself as I leaned away from the voice. *Fran.* "Wh – what are you doing here?" I managed, staring up at her with fear curdling in my stomach. I felt as though I might actually vomit all over her pretty suede boots.

She took a step forward, reaching out as though she might touch my cheek, but I cringed away from her. She gave a sad little smile. "I saw your trainers were gone and assumed you'd be here. I was worried about you," she shrugged. "You never came up to bed last night." She sat down beside me on the bench and I turned to face her, not because I wanted to see her, but because I was afraid to turn my back on her. What a sad situation we'd arrived at.

"Fran," I said, squeezing my hands into fists to stop them from shaking. "I think we both know what has to happen. I'm going to pack my stuff today. I'm going to stay with Brett or Matt until I can find somewhere to rent."

"What? Why?"

"Are you joking? Look at me, Fran! Look at the state of my face."

She rolled her eyes. "Oh, that? I thought you were into it? You seemed to be having fun."

"You crossed a line. I think that's obvious."

She shook her head, leaning closer, touching my knee and I jerked it out of her reach. "You can't pretend to be some weak little boy, Josh. You could have stopped me if you weren't enjoying it." She laughed suddenly. "I mean, look at me! I'm not even half your size. You would have stopped me if you didn't want me to do it, I know you would have," she said with a teasing smile. "This is really silly, Josh. Just come home and I'll make you breakfast. There are sausages in the fridge. And mushrooms."

I shook my head. "No. I'm sorry but I can't. I can't let you just brush this under the carpet. You hurt me. On purpose," I added, though speaking the words out loud was far more difficult than I could ever have imagined. It was humiliating to admit that my girlfriend had beaten me up, but that was exactly what had happened and I couldn't let her deny it. "You meant to punish me for going to the ceremony, and now look at me! How am I supposed to explain this to my friends?"

She shrugged, though her eyes wouldn't meet mine. I could tell she wasn't happy about discussing the events of last night. It was embarrassing for her to have to see the consequences of her actions in the cold light of day. "Just... oh, I don't know. Tell them you got in a fight or something."

"So, lie? You want me to lie to my friends and pretend you had nothing to do with this?" I sighed, looking down at my feet. "Can't you hear yourself, Fran? Can't you see how fucked up this whole situation is? You can't just lay into me like this!"

"But... but I can't have hurt you, Josh. Not really... and if I did, well, I'm sorry, okay? I didn't mean to... I was just playing, just messing around," she said. She looked scared now. *Good*. That meant she was finally taking me seriously.

"You took it way too far. I'm sorry, Fran, but I won't live in fear of you – "

"Fear? You can't be serious? Just look at the size of me compared to you! Of course you aren't afraid of me. How can you even say that?" I stared at her, feeling confused and angry with myself. I didn't want to back down. My decision was made. But she really did look genuinely surprised at how seriously I was taking my injuries. "Josh, I'm – I'm sorry, okay? I didn't realise. I got wrapped up in the excitement, I guess. But you're right, I took it too far. Please, say you'll stay? I promise it won't happen again. I swear, we'll forget it ever happened."

"I don't think I can."

She leaned forward, grabbing my hands between hers and I was surprised to see her eyes shimmering with tears. "Please, Josh? You and me are so good together. I *love* you. I would never do anything to hurt you intentionally. I just didn't realise my own strength. I didn't think I could do anything to really hurt you. You're so big, Josh. I didn't realise!" she sobbed.

I hated when she cried. I could feel it melting my resolve. Seeing her looking up at me with her wide, innocent eyes, her cheeks flushed with emotion at the prospect of losing what we had, it was ridiculous to think I could ever be afraid of her. She was so sweet and small and lovely. She needed me to keep her safe. And maybe she was right. She'd just got over excited and lost herself in the moment. Maybe role-playing could do that to a person.

I swallowed thickly, letting her rest her head against my chest, my body relaxing as she leaned against me. I sighed and looked down, brushing her hair from her face. She stared up at me, waiting and I knew she'd broken me. "You promise, it won't happen again?" I asked, holding her close.

"Yes," she whispered through a choked sob. "It won't happen again. I promise, Josh."

"Okay." I kissed her on the forehead and stood up, holding out a hand to her. "Then let's go home."

Chapter Seventeen

Kaitlyn

I looked up, breathless as Marcus walked purposefully into the room, smiling victoriously as his gaze landed on me. "You made it. Good."

I nodded. I'd been up half the night wondering how to manage Rex, the school, the children who were making his life hell, *and* make it into work for eight a.m. as Marcus had instructed. I'd crafted a long, detailed email to the head of the school, detailing my expectations for his response to the bullying situation, hoping my no nonsense tone would spur him into finally taking action. But still, I knew it would take days, if not weeks for anything to be put in place. It wasn't like I hadn't been in on numerous other occasions, waiting outside Mr. Clarkson's door like I'd been summoned for a telling off myself. I'd already decided that I would go in wearing my uniform next time. It might make him take me more seriously. But in the meantime, I couldn't bring myself to send my sweet boy back there. It would be the cruellest thing I could possibly do to him, and I knew I would never forgive myself if he was hurt again.

In the end, I'd called the childminder, begging her to take Rex for the day. It would mean handing over nearly a full days pay to her so that I could avoid having to miss work, but it was my only option. It showed just how dire the situation was that Rex had agreed to spend a day surrounded by snotty, half-naked toddlers in sodden nappies rather than go to school, but at least for now, I knew he was safe.

"Any news on the Jones case, Guv?" I asked, wanting to get right down to business. I was still put out by his suggestion that I pandered to Rex by not letting him be beaten to a pulp by the school bullies. "Have they found the baby boy?" I asked hopefully.

"Not yet."

"Okay. I take it we're questioning Mr. Jones again this morning?"

Marcus shook his head and sighed. "No. He's still at the hospital, and I've just heard from them. They want us to come in."

"To the hospital?" I asked in surprise.

"Apparently they have some interesting developments they want to tell us about in person."

"What does that mean? He's confessed?"

Marcus shrugged. "I don't think so. I'd expected him to be brought back here during the night. Was quite the surprise to find out he was still there when I arrived this morning. No idea what they're playing at – I bet he's pulling a fast one. They don't usually keep you in overnight for a broken wrist, do they?" he said wryly, fixing me with a piercing stare as if he expected me to have all the answers. He unfolded his arms and checked his watch, the fake gold strap glinting in the thick thatch of wiry grey arm hair. "We won't find out what's going on hanging around here, though, will we? You ready?"

I glanced at the clock, hoping Rex was okay. "Yep," I answered, moving to the door as he held it open for me. "Let's go."

The hospital ward smelled like burned toast and stale urine, the tang of disinfectant growing stronger as we made our way past the toilets, pressing our bodies close to the wall to allow a pair of porters pushing a woman on a narrow bed, to move past us. The woman smiled at me, her knuckles white as she gripped the bars of the gurney, her pupils round with fear, despite her sunny expression. We moved on, past the visitor's room where several people sat silently, each in their own secluded bubble of tension, clutching their mugs of tea like a shield as they awaited news of loved ones.

A nurse holding a tray containing a single syringe and an alcohol wipe paused as she saw us, and whispered something to the woman behind the desk, who stood, waving her away. The dark blue uniform signifying her role as the ward Sister hung loosely over her wiry frame, her frizzy red hair pinned back close to her head. She was tight lipped and fidgety as if she had a thousand things to be getting on with, and I knew she wouldn't waste time making small talk. She understood what it meant to be busy.

Marcus stepped forward, holding out his hand for her to shake. "You're expecting us?"

"Yes, follow me." She led us down a narrow

corridor and into a side room where a nurse was eating a bowl of cereal, her eyes glued to her phone screen. "Verity, sorry, I need you to leave for a bit," the Sister said briskly, holding the door open pointedly. I saw the weary frustration at having her breakfast disturbed and felt sorry for the young girl who no doubt had ten of her twelve hour shift left, and one of her precious breaks disturbed by our presence. She didn't complain though. She placed her half eaten meal on the counter and slipped her phone into her pocket, nodding deferentially as she slipped out of the staff room.

The Sister pushed the door closed and turned to face us. "Mr. Jones," she said, plaiting her fingers in front of her as if she were conducting a presentation, "has significant injuries. He has a serious concussion, a head wound that has required multiple stitches, a fractured wrist and several broken ribs. He is deficient in iron and vitamin D, he has bruises of varying ages covering his torso and he has several scars on his body and limbs which suggest he has been cut on numerous occasions. He also has scars which look very much like burns from cigarettes on the soles of his feet." She took a deep breath, her eyes flicking between Marcus and me.

"It is, of course, not my job to determine the origins of his injuries, but to treat them. However, I feel it only right to say that in my professional opinion, this man has been the victim of physical abuse, dating back several years, if not more. I have seen it before, and it's hard to fathom what else could have caused his injuries." She stared at us, waiting and I looked to Marcus who was shaking his head.

He gave an incredulous cough. "You're suggesting he's been abused? By who, his *wife?*"

"That *is* the most likely scenario, wouldn't you agree?" the Sister said, with a raised eyebrow. "Anyway, I'll give you both a moment to have a chat and then I'll take you to see him. Okay?"

"Yes," I agreed. "That will be fine." I waited for the click of the door as she left, then turned to Marcus. "Wow."

He pursed his lips and I saw the angry flicker of his moustache. "She is mistaken. I went to the house after you left yesterday, then to the morgue. I saw the body. His wife is *tiny,* Kaitlyn. She's a waif, for god's sake. And Joshua Jones looks like he'd have a shot at winning the world heavyweight championship. It's impossible."

"Not impossible," I said, lowering myself onto the arm of the grey sofa. It was hard and uncomfortable. "It happens, Guv. Men being the victim rather than the perp."

"Yeah, *weak* men. Scrawny guys with no backbone. Not men like him. He's a fireman! Not some weak little git who'd let a bloody woman walk all over him. It's laughable, Kait. He'd snap her like a twig."

I bit my tongue, refusing to take the bait on his sexist remarks. "Well, perhaps he did? I mean, couldn't it be possible that he put up with her hurting him for so long, that he just snapped? Fought back and stabbed her in a fit of rage that had been building for years?"

"Because she'd been abusing him?" Marcus sneered. "Nope, I can't go with that. If you'd have seen her, you'd understand. You wouldn't give it a second thought."

"Then who hurt him? *Who?* I think you're being hasty, Guv. You've got to consider this. We don't know anything about the wife yet. Maybe she was stronger in other ways? That's how abusers work, isn't it? They break you down. Make you weak mentally before they ever lay a finger on you. If she was stronger mentally, smarter than him even, she could – "

"No, Kaitlyn. It's ridiculous. A male being the victim of domestic abuse is so rare as it is, let alone with a man the size of Joshua Jones. It's not possible."

"*Is* it rare, though?" I argued, feeling the frustration building within me. "Or is it just that men are too afraid to ask for help for fear they'd get a response like the one you're giving now?" I asked, aware that my voice was growing steadily louder. Marcus glared at me and I glared back, unwilling to back down. The door opened and the Sister stood there, taking in the tense scene in front of her. To her credit, she didn't mention it.

"I can take you to see him now," she said. "Come this way." I tore my eyes away from Marcus's accusing stare and followed after her.

The man reclining in the hospital bed clad in the thin cream gown, his eyes downcast towards his lap, looked nothing like the man I'd met at the police-station yesterday morning. He seemed to have diminished in size, his shoulders curved in, his whole demeanour shrunken. He glanced up as we passed the constable guarding his door and I made a mental note that he'd been given a private room. His eyes seemed to travel over Marcus's face, then mine, before lowering to the thin blue blanket covering his body.

I stepped in front of Marcus before he could speak. He'd put *me* on the job, and now that I'd seen how closed-minded he was being, I wasn't going to give up the reins without a fight. "Josh," I said, stepping closer. "How are you feeling?"

He glanced up in surprise, then gave a shrug. "That's a strange question to ask someone in my position," he said softly. He made a small sound in the back of his throat, and swallowed audibly. "Broken. That's how I'm feeling. Completely broken."

"The ward Sister tells me your wrist and head injuries will heal nicely."

He gave a sudden burst of laughter, his dark eyes meeting mine. "That... wasn't what I meant. My *son*. My baby boy. Have you found him yet?" he asked, tears filling his eyes, spilling over, trickling down his cheeks. He continued to stare at me without a trace of embarrassment. "I need to see him. To say goodbye."

"I don't think – " Marcus began.

I cut in, flashing Marcus a glance I hoped would silence him. "We have people looking now, but no. We haven't found him yet." Marcus made an annoying clicking sound with his tongue and I resisted the urge to tell him to leave us in peace. "Mr. Jones, can you tell me how you got your injuries?" I asked, maintaining eye contact, though I could tell he was uncomfortable. He sucked in a breath, staring at me and I bit my lip, determined not to speak, to break the

153

spell. I couldn't hold him though. His eyes slid away from my face and I knew the moment was over.

"I can't," he whispered through a thick veil of tears. "I just can't. I'm sorry."

"Did your wife do this? Did she hurt you, Josh?" He continued to stare down at the bed, the silence stretching on. "I need your help, Josh. If you can tell us *anything*, anything at all, it may help our search team to locate your son. That's what you want, isn't it? For us to find him?" I leaned forward, lowering my voice. "Did your wife do something to the baby, Josh? Please, tell me what happened."

Josh gave a choked sob and dropped his head into his hands. "I'm sorry. I can't.... I just can't."

The Sister stepped in front of me, her expression blank and unreadable. "I think that will do. My patient has a serious head injury and needs to rest."

"Your patient?" Marcus said. "I think you mean our suspect."

"You can ask your questions when he's in a fit state to answer them," she replied, her voice firm and unwavering. "But right now, his health and recovery are my priorities. So off you go." Marcus opened his mouth to argue but I held out a hand, cutting him off. To my surprise, it worked.

"Thank you for your time. And Mr. Jones, if you think of anything at all that can help us, or if you have anything you'd like to tell us, anything at all, you can inform whichever constable is at your door and we'll come straight here. And I do mean anything," I said meaningfully. "You and I have plenty we can be getting on with," I said to Marcus. "Let's not waste time." He gave a reluctant nod and flashed a furious glance at Josh, clearly still convinced he was pulling a fast one to avoid sleeping in a cell. It was far more pleasant getting the hospital treatment.

"He did it. I'm sure of it," Marcus growled as we made our way back through the ward. "Did you see those crocodile tears? The guy's playing us for fools and you're falling for it. I thought you were stronger than this, Kaitlyn, I wouldn't have given you the time of day otherwise."

"I'm strong enough. But I think you're wrong."

"You don't think he's guilty?"

I looked over my shoulder to where the PC stood guarding his door. "No," I said, shaking my head slowly. "I don't."

Chapter Eighteen

Kaitlyn

Marcus had been off with me all afternoon, griping about the *'woman's touch'* he'd been so keen on when he'd roped me into sitting in on the case. Forensics had cleared out of the house and the post-mortem had been rushed through and was currently underway, but despite the search team's best efforts, we still had no idea where the baby was. We'd found out several things about the tight knit little family of three though.

The wife, Franchesca, had been a scientist, highly regarded in her field and had taken less than two weeks maternity leave, a fact that had nearly made me spit out my tea in surprise when I'd heard it. Their finances looked healthy enough, and although as a fireman, Josh was clearly the lower earner of the two, it still stunned me that *he'd* been the one to take paternity leave and stay home with the baby when he was still so very new to the world. I couldn't imagine choosing to miss out on such a special time. Those early months with a newborn were precious, I wouldn't have given them up for the world.

The baby, Edwin Jones, had been born less than six weeks previously and since being discharged from hospital, had been seen by nobody outside the couple. Several of Franchesca's colleagues mentioned that she hadn't wanted to discuss the baby on returning to work, preferring to get right back to her usual routine as if nothing had changed, and a few had said they didn't know she was pregnant at all, echoing the words of her neighbours.

There seemed to be some confusion amongst her team over whether she'd changed her mind over coming back so soon. She'd applied for leave shortly after returning from having the baby, unwilling to give a reason, and fearing rebuttal if he refused, her boss had granted it.

None of the people interviewed had offered any kind of emotional response, according to the officers who had interviewed them. No tears. No outbursts of grief. It seemed that Franchesca had very few people who actually knew and cared about her, which made the ward Sister's theory of abuse even more likely.

Had Josh snapped? It wasn't unheard of. Granted, when these stories were in the papers, it was always the wife who'd been pushed too far too many times. *"I cut his throat while he was sleeping after years of torture." "I hit him with a pan of boiling water when he tried to rape me again."*

Those were the sordid headlines people were used to seeing. But that didn't mean that it didn't happen to men too. Josh was a puzzle. The more I learned about him, the more I believed there was so much more he was hiding from us.

We'd discovered, just this afternoon, that he'd been awarded the Queen's Gallantry Medal for bravery having risked his life to save a little girl in a house fire. His boss, Mike Murphy had called the station in tears having been visited by a couple of PC's, listing every merit under the sun, telling us vehemently how selfless, how generous, how much of a perfect gentleman Joshua Jones was and as the day passed, we'd had calls from others who had heard the news, determined to defend him too.

"So he's perfect, is that it?" Marcus sneered as I relayed a call from a woman he'd pulled out of the wreckage of a major train crash six years previously.

"Of course not. Nobody is. But what we're hearing doesn't add up, Guv. You have to admit, he isn't your typical murderer."

"Do I?" Marcus grunted. I could tell he was irritable because I was right. "Be that as it may, you're forgetting something. We have a dead woman and a missing baby, who he's told us himself is also dead. *Somebody* killed them, Kaitlyn. If not him, then who?"

"I don't know. I was under the impression it was our job to find out."

"Don't push your luck, Kaitlyn. Look, I'll accept that he's been labelled the local hero. I'll even let him be cast as the good guy if it makes you happy. But good guys can be pushed too far too, you know? Let's say you're right... about the abuse, not that I can believe it, but for arguments sake. Maybe Franchesca Jones was a nightmare to live with. Moaning all the time, making him stay home with the baby rather than go back to work with his mates, making his life a misery, as wives so often do."

I bit my lip, holding back a strong desire to throw his glass of orange juice right in his smug face. "Maybe she came home one night and the baby had been crying all day, and she started bitching and moaning about the state of the house and he just lost it? Shook the baby to death then stabbed her, out of sheer frustration. Then, realising what he'd done, he comes here, makes no sense whatsoever then refuses to speak another word about it? Isn't that a plausible chain of events?"

I shook my head slowly. "No. Maybe, if it had just been the wife. *Maybe*. But killing his son? *His child?* I can't see it. And I can't understand why he would pretend not to know where the baby was. If he did it, he'd know, wouldn't he? Guv, you *saw* how cut up he was over it. I just can't believe that a man so used to high pressure situations, a man who'd run into a burning building to save a little girl, could be capable of this. I don't believe it."

"You'd be surprised what people can be capable of, Kaitlyn. The secrets they keep behind closed doors. Just because you don't believe it, doesn't mean it's not true."

I was still replaying the conversation with Marcus as I ran through Sarah's front gate at gone six p.m. I could hear music playing from inside and cringed as I realised it was Rihanna. Making a mental note to buy her some more appropriate children's CDs from the charity shop when I got paid, I pressed the bell and waited for the sound of footsteps as she made her way to the door, a cornetto in one hand, a crying baby propped against her shoulder. Her eyes widened as if she were surprised to see me. "Oh, Kaitlyn, right yes, I'm expecting you aren't I?" she blustered. "I think Rex is upstairs. Come in for a sec."

"You *think?*"

"It's been one of those days. This one hasn't stopped bawling since his grandma dropped him off first thing," she sighed, patting the red faced baby ineffectually. "I think Rex fancied himself a bit of peace and quiet, if there's such a thing to be found in this house. Rexy!" she yelled up the stairs. "Mum's here!" She waited a moment and tutted. "Doubt he can hear me over this racket. I'll go up."

"I'll go," I said, stepping towards the stairs. "That is, if you don't mind?"

"Nah, you go for it. I need to warm a bottle anyway. Just got a text to say this one's not getting picked up for another hour. Makes you wonder why they bother having kids if they never see the poor things, don't it?" she said, pushing the front door closed. Catching the horrified look on my face she flushed. "Oh, I don't mean *you,* love. You're doing your best. I just mean – "

I held up a hand. "It doesn't matter. Look, I'm tired and it's been a very long day. I'll just nip up and get him if you don't mind?"

Sarah nodded and stepped back, still clearly embarrassed by her blunder. I climbed the creaky stairs, listening for sounds of life as I reached the landing. There a towering pile of hastily folded laundry propped beside the bathroom door, an old grey cat fast asleep in the pieces that had fallen to the carpet. I pushed open the closest door to see Sarah's unmade double bed, the chest of drawers covered in half empty coffee mugs, the curtains only slightly cracked open. The TV was on in the corner, the sound muted, an old episode of *Friends* casting a ghostly glow over the room.

I pulled the door shut and turned to the next room. "Rex?" I called softly. I opened the door and peered around it. Rex was sitting in a shabby armchair beside the window, his knees pulled up to his chest, a picture book that was far too young to hold his attention strewn at his feet. Slowly, as if he were waking from a long, deep sleep, he turned to look at me. Then, without a word, he hauled himself up.

"Hi, sweetie, did you... has today been okay?" I asked softly. "I – I wanted to call at lunchtime but I ran out of time."

"Doesn't matter," he shrugged, looking at his feet.

"Rex, has something happened today? Why are you up here, all alone?" He shrugged again. "Rex?" I pushed.

"It's *fine,* Mum. It's not like it would make a difference anyway, would it?" he said, still not looking me in the eye. His words caught me off guard, the jaded accusations of an angry teenager, not the innocent, trusting voice that should have come from a child. But his anger was a front. I could see that as clear as day. He wasn't experienced enough to hide his true feelings. He tried to give off a vibe of nonchalance, but he just looked so sad. So very alone. I wanted to reach out and pull him into my arms, but something stopped me. The fear that he was finally beginning to blame me for all of this. I'd done my best, but it had never been enough. It had never helped to fix things and give him back the life he'd once loved.

"Let's go," I said quietly, holding open the door. He didn't argue. He walked through it in sullen silence and I called goodbye to Sarah, not waiting for her to emerge from the kitchen. We walked back through the estate in tense silence. A few streets away from home, I stopped, placing a hand on his shoulder, waiting for him to look at me. To my relief, he didn't shrug me away. It took a moment, but when he eventually looked up, the expression on his face was like a knife to my gut. "It won't always be this way, Rex. I know it's so hard right now. And I know you miss how things were. I do too."

"I hate Dad for leaving."

I bit my lip, unsure what I was supposed to say to that. I didn't want my sweet little boy to be consumed by hatred, corroded from the inside out by his anger, his hurt at being rejected by the one man who should have never let him down. But how could I tell him to forgive and forget when I'd been unable to do it myself? I hated Mitch too. And for the nights of tears and days of terror he'd caused my son, I didn't think I would ever find the strength to forgive him. I sighed. "There's a chance I might get a new position at work... a promotion. The interview is at the end of the week and if I *do* get it, we'll have a bit more money. Mummy will have better hours so we can spend more time together, like we used to."

"And we can move?" he asked, a flash of hope crossing his pale little face.

"Oh yes, we can move."

He thought for a moment. "But what if you don't

get the job? What then?"

I stared at him, wishing I had the answers. "We'll cross that bridge when we come to it. Come on, it's time we had some dinner."

We crossed the road, walking back to our flat and I fished around inside my pocket for the keys. There was a strong smell of damp in the air as we entered, and a distant tang of weed that I chose to ignore. The post table was crammed with letters and I rifled through them, hoping mine hadn't been stolen again. My heart sank as I counted out the bills with my name on, the angry red letters emblazoned across the pristine white envelopes. No matter how much overtime I did, how little I spent, there was never enough. We were sinking faster than I could bail us out, and I didn't know how to scrape my way back into the black.

"Mummy?"

"One sec, Rex," I said, trying to compose myself before he could see my fear.

"Mummy, *look.*"

I glanced over my shoulder to see Rex looking up

at the door to our flat, his lips quivering as he stared at the bright red spray painted message defacing our home. *Fuck Off Pig!* "Oh," I whispered. Somehow, despite keeping myself to myself, never wearing my uniform without a coat to hide it, somebody had figured out who and what I was. In a place like this, it was only a matter of time before they all knew. How safe would we be then? How long before they came hammering at our door to demand justice for their friends who'd been on the wrong side of the law?

I pushed back my shoulders, shaking my head at Rex. "That's a silly message," I tutted. "What a mess. We'll just have to paint over it, won't we?" I said brightly, flashing him a reassuring smile. "I think a nice green colour, don't you?"

"I know what it means, Mummy."

"I – do you?"

"Yes. It means now we aren't safe anywhere. Not at school and *not* at home. One way or another, the bad people will get us." And with that, he burst into noisy tears.

Chapter Nineteen

Josh

I couldn't stop smiling. Not only had Franchesca agreed to come to Brett and Millie's house-warming party, but she was by far the most beautiful woman in the room and I could feel the eyes of everyone we passed as we moved through the crowd, laughing and mingling. Franchesca was on top form, the very best version of herself, the witty, sharp, funny woman who managed to make everyone fall in love with her. It had been four months since the award ceremony incident, and though we'd had our disagreements, Fran had kept her word, for the most part.

I tried not to think too much about the occasions when she'd slipped. The few times she'd broken my things in a rage, or her increasing habit of throwing away my dinner when I was still trying to eat it. She would slam the bin lid down and look at me with challenging eyes, daring me to go to the fridge and get a snack. I couldn't deal with the conflict. It was easier to go to bed hungry than push her when she was in those moods. But she hadn't hit me again. She hadn't let herself give into that level of extremity. That was the main thing.

For such a long time now, I'd felt as if my life had been carved down the middle. Fran always seemed to come up with an excuse for not coming out with my friends, and more often than not, I ended up cancelling too out of guilt. It wasn't as if I could go to the pub with my workmates when she'd sprained her ankle or had a stomach-ache, so while the rest of my team were off playing darts over cold beers, I would be at home massaging Fran's feet and fending off increasingly pissed off texts from Mike and Brett.

Both of them were in relationships and yet I knew that Millie and Lara were only too happy to tag along on nights out with the team, or to make their own plans without a fuss. I'd been beginning to wonder if Fran and I were in such a private little bubble that we'd fallen into a trap of co-dependence. We were isolating ourselves. I knew it, only every time I tried to bring it up, Fran somehow managed to spin it into a positive thing, telling me we were lucky to be so in love. That we didn't need anyone but each other. It was sweet, but all the same, I couldn't deny how refreshing it was to have all my favourite people under one roof for a change tonight.

I whispered in her ear, offering her a top up and she smiled sweetly, holding out her glass in response. It was at times like these I had no doubt about where we were heading. All the rough patches, her mood swings and her tendency to lash out when she didn't get her own way seemed to fade into the background, and all I could see was the woman of my dreams.

I weaved my way through the packed living room, heading for the kitchen. Before I reached the door, I felt a hand clamp round my wrist, gripping tightly. My stomach dropped instantly, my hands beginning to tremble in horrible anticipation. I turned slowly, and let out a deep sigh of relief.

"Well, well, well, look who made it to the party," Rebecca grinned, releasing my wrist and slapping me playfully on the shoulder. "Jesus, Josh are you ill or something? You're all pale and sweaty!"

I shook my head, wiping my damp brow with my

shirt sleeve. "I'm fine." I tried to force a smile. Over Rebecca's shoulder I saw Fran glance our way, her eyes narrowing. I took a step back from Rebecca, not wanting to give Fran any reason to feel jealous. When I looked her way again, she had turned her back on us and was talking animatedly with a group of guests.

"So," Rebecca said, her eyebrow arching as she met my eyes. "How have you been, Josh? I mean, I hardly see you these days. I can't remember the last time we were even on shift together, let alone when you last made it out with us. I thought we were friends, Josh?"

I bowed my head, unable to hold eye contact with her. I didn't want to tell her the truth – that it had been me who had done the rotas for the next quarter and I'd purposefully made sure that she and I would cross paths as little as possible so that Franchesca would give me a break. I liked Rebecca. She'd always been a good, solid friend, funny, deep and completely reliable when it came to the job. If I were honest with myself, I missed her and I resented that I was having to lose so many people in my life in order to placate my girlfriend. But, as Fran had pointed out, there weren't many women who'd be happy to let their partners carry on as they had in their single life. Every relationship came with compromises, and this was just one of mine.

"Of course we're friends," I said, flashing her a grin. "Life's just a bit hectic right now. You know how it is. Everything okay with you?" I added in a rush, increasingly aware of how long I'd been standing with her. Fran might not be looking, but I knew she was hyper aware of my every move. There was no way she would let this slide.

"I'm okay," she shrugged. "I've been a bit under the weather lately, actually – "

"Oh, that's a shame, sorry to hear that. Glad to see you're all better now. Look, sorry, Bex, I've gotta go. Promised Fran I'd get her a top up."

"Course you did." Her smile faded. I pretended not to see the sadness in her eyes as I turned for the door.

I poured the wine hastily, slopping it over the edge of the glass in my angst to get back to

Franchesca. I wanted to go back in there and pretend everything was alright. There was no reason for it *not* to be alright, I'd done nothing wrong. But the queasy feeling in the pit of my stomach reminded me that Fran wouldn't see it that way. She would see my talking to another woman as a betrayal. A snub.

I rushed back to the living room, taking a convoluted path around the edge of the crowd so as not to come anywhere close to Rebecca again. Fran was standing with her back to me, chatting to a tall blonde man in a pink shirt and pressed blue jeans. As I approached, I heard Fran's light, tinkling laughter, saw the way she reached out, touching his forearm. I sidled up beside her and held out her glass. "Here you go, Franchesca. Sorry for the delay."

She stared down at the wine glass as if it were filled with writhing maggots and it was only then I realised she was already holding a drink. "You seemed to be rather too distracted to deal with my needs, so Christopher here brought me one." She raised the glass to her lips, taking a slow sip, her eyes drifting away from my face as she looked flirtatiously up at the stranger. I didn't recognise him as one of Brett's friends. He had to be a guest of Millie's.

I felt a surge of irritation but swallowed it down, shrugging nonchalantly. "No harm done. I'll have it myself." I took a swig of the tart white wine, wishing it was lager instead, then held out a hand. "Chris, is it? I'm Josh."

"Pleasure," he drawled, flashing an inquisitive glance at Fran. She smiled and gave a tiny shake of her head, as if denying her connection to me, and I felt suddenly small and insignificant, despite the fact I probably had three stone of muscle on the guy.

"We were just discussing the situation in Calais. The refugees," Franchesca added. She turned her attention back to Christopher. "Joshua likes to stick his head in the sand when it comes to the news. Hasn't a clue what's going on outside London, have you, Josh?" she added with a vindictive laugh.

"Well, that's not strictly true," I said, gripping my glass a little tighter in my sweating palm. "I just don't like to immerse myself in it. It's all so negative."

Christopher laughed. "You don't look like the

sensitive type. Find it too upsetting, is that it? My mum's the same."

"I expect it's more a case of not understanding what's being said," Fran said in a stage whisper. "Brains and beauty were too much to ask for." I stared at her, shocked at her cruelty.

"Not in your case," Christopher said, not missing an opportunity to flatter her. What kind of snake was he, sliding in, trying to steal her right in front of me? Franchesca smiled graciously, her eyes not leaving his. Did she really think she could treat me like this? Like her little pet? Like fucking dirt! I knew exactly why she was being this way. Because of Rebecca. Because I'd dared to make small talk with a member of the opposite sex rather than snub her publicly.

Fran ran her hand down Christopher's arm, making a transparent comment about the quality of the material of his shirt, her fingers pressing lightly, lingering too long. She was trying to humiliate me. To embarrass me in front of my friends and I wasn't going to take it. I would never dream of doing this to her, making her feel so damn insignificant. Without a word, I turned away, heading blindly for the kitchen. I had to get away from her before I snapped. I didn't want to ruin Brett's party, or have my relationship be the gossip everyone remembered from tonight. I grabbed the closest bottle of spirits from the kitchen table, spinning the lid loose, swigging the burning alcohol back straight from the bottle. I grimaced as I pulled back, looking at the label. *Rum*. Disgusting. But as I grasped the bottle with shaking hands, I realised it had given me a new lease of courage. I was a good man. A *decent* man. But I wasn't a pushover and I would not let my girlfriend punish me for a crime I hadn't committed. I put the bottle back on the table, determined and ready. I would march back in there and tell her we were going home, so we could discuss this without an audience, and without posh twats lurking nearby like scavengers ready to pick at the pieces of our relationship. I couldn't keep letting Franchesca walk all over me like this. I wouldn't be thrown aside, expected to wait quietly and take my punishment like a whipped puppy. Not anymore.

"Hey, who was that posh guy Fran was with?"

Brett asked, coming into the kitchen, glancing at the bottle of rum clenched in my palm.

"I don't know. Some guy called Christopher. I thought he was a friend of Millie's?"

"Maybe, but your girlfriend seems to know him better. She just left with the guy."

"What? She left?"

"Yeah, a few minutes ago. Did you two have a row or something?"

I shook my head, speechless. "She can't have left. She wouldn't just go – not without talking to me. Did she say where she was going to?"

"No, mate." He stepped forward, placing a hand on my shoulder and I shrugged it off. I didn't want his pity. "What's going on?" Brett asked, frowning.

I shook my head. "I wish I knew. Was – was she okay?" I asked suddenly. What if he'd dropped something in her drink? Some date rape drug. That would make sense.

"How do you mean?" Brett frowned.

"Sober. Did she look drunk? Was she stumbling? Slurring?"

"She was fine, mate. I watched her put her coat on and hug Millie goodbye. She walked out on her own two feet."

"I have to go after her." I pushed past him, running to the front door, throwing it open. I sprinted onto the street, looking up and down it, seeing nothing but an old lady pushing her shopping trolley.

"I'm sure it's nothing," Brett said, coming up behind me. "I mean, you two are solid, right?"

"Yeah," I said, swallowing thickly. "We're good."

Chapter Twenty

Josh

I'd had long nights before. Those never ending shifts where every time I laid my head down on the pillow, another emergency call would come in. Times when I would rush from one minor incident to another, never getting a chance to stop and catch my breath. But last night had been so much worse. There was nothing to do. Nothing to keep my mind occupied. I had no idea where Franchesca might be, and tempted as I might have been, I knew I couldn't call the police. She was a grown woman who had left of her own accord with another man. It would have actually been easier if I'd been able to report her missing or abducted. But she had chosen this. All I could do was wait, and hope she came back.

At some point in the early hours of the morning, I must have fallen asleep on the sofa, but the sound of a key in the front door roused me instantly and I pulled myself upright, rubbing the sleep from my eyes. The clock on the mantelpiece read 10.14 a.m.

She'd stayed with him the whole night.

I sat, frozen, unsure what to do now that she was actually here. I'd played the scene a thousand times in my head throughout the night, changing both my response and hers. I would cry. She would. I'd tell her I was leaving. She'd lash out and hurt me. Or worse, she'd let me go. Now that she was here, I was terrified to move. To play the scene for real.

I heard her slow footsteps moving down the hall towards me. The living room door swung open and I raised my head, looking up at her, my stomach contracting in longing, disgust, hurt and fear. Our eyes met and it took all my strength not to jump up and run across the room, to hold her in my arms and thank her for coming back to me. But I wouldn't do it. I was better than that.

"Josh," she whispered, and I realised she was crying. "Oh, Josh, I've done something terrible."

"You slept with him."

She nodded. "Yes."

"Why?" I whispered. "Why would you throw away everything we had for one night?"

She gave a choked sob and gripped the door-frame, her fingers shaking. My body moved without my say so, rising to my feet, striding towards her and taking her elbow as I guided her back to the sofa. She gave a grateful little smile and I gritted my teeth, hating that I'd been unable to fight the ingrained chivalry. I let go of her and moved to sit at the far end of the sofa, putting several feet of distance between us, though I half wanted to offer her a glass of water.

"I was jealous. And afraid," she sniffed, shaking her head. "I saw you talking to Rebecca. The way she was looking at you. There's something between you both. I know there is."

"You're wrong."

"I'm not. I know she likes you, Josh. And when I saw you talking, I was just so scared."

"So you decided to go home with another man?"

"To play you at your own game," she said softly.

"Right. Only I never slept with Rebecca. I barely said two words to her, did I? I've never even thought of cheating on you, Fran!"

"I know, I know. Oh god, Josh, I don't know what I was thinking. You're the best thing that's ever happened to me and it scares me. I've never had someone like you in my life. It's like it's too good to be true. I'm so afraid it's only temporary. I know you'll leave me, sooner or later. You're too good for me. You really are." Fat tears were rolling down her cheeks, making her look so fragile, so vulnerable. It made me feel protective. I shook off the feeling.

"Do you have any idea how much it hurt to realise you'd left with him? Can you imagine how that felt, Fran?"

"I'm so sorry. I really am. I pushed you away because I was scared of losing you, and now I've done that anyway. I've ruined everything, haven't I?" She covered her face with her hands, her shoulders heaving. She looked so pitiful, so very sad.

"You haven't lost me," I heard myself say.

"What?"

I sighed. "You made a mistake. A stupid, hurtful mistake. But you won't repeat it. Will you?"

"No. Never."

"Then let's put it to bed."

"You'll stay?"

"Yes. I'll stay."

She launched herself across the sofa, gripping my neck, her damp cheek pressed against mine. "You won't leave me? Promise, you'll never leave me, Josh. No matter what. We'll always be together. Promise me that, Josh."

"I promise," I said into her hair, knowing it was true. "I won't ever leave you, Fran. I couldn't if I tried."

Chapter Twenty-One

Josh

"You're what?"

Franchesca placed the canvas shopping bag on the kitchen counter, unpacking eggs and bread and bananas, bustling from one cupboard to another without pausing to look at me. "How's that new coffee? Good?" she asked over her shoulder.

"Franchesca!"

She sighed dramatically, slamming a tin of beans into a cupboard, knocking over a packet of pasta so it cascaded down over the counter. "Don't get yourself worked up over it, Josh. I'm not going to keep it." She flung the cupboard shut, ignoring the mess and turned towards me, a brittle smile on her face.

I didn't know what to think. "Fran, if you're pregnant with my child, I think I have – "

"Ha! Don't, Joshua. Just don't, okay?"

"Don't what?"

"Give me *the talk*. Tell me you want it. You know I'm not maternal."

"You never said you didn't want kids. I mean, I always thought we would have our own someday. I thought that was where we were heading." I placed my coffee down on the edge of the counter. Fran stared at me, open mouthed and then she let rip with a sudden laugh, a cold, cruel laugh that held no joy in it. It was clearly at my expense, though I had no idea why.

"You seriously think we could be parents? Can you picture it, Josh? I mean, really?"

I considered her question. The truth was, I couldn't picture her cooing over a baby. I couldn't imagine her changing nappies or reading bedtime stories, let alone getting up at night to sooth a hungry baby. Fran liked her freedom, and the slightest interruption to her sleep made her out of sorts for days afterwards. These days, if I was on call at night, I had to sleep downstairs on the lumpy sofa. We had a perfectly good spare room, but she wouldn't allow me to use it incase my footsteps on the landing disturbed her precious sleep.

Motherhood wouldn't come easily to her. It would

be a challenge. But there was a chance that a child would soften her sharp corners. Help her to become more grounded. Franchesca may not be typical mother material, but I knew that I could make up for anything she lacked. I could be a good father. More than good. The idea of having a child, *my* child, to shower with love, made my eyes sting and my heart swell. I didn't have to try to picture it – the image burned bright in my mind. "Don't get rid of our baby," I said, my voice ringing with a sense of conviction that was alien to me. "We can make this work, Fran. We can be a family."

She threw back her head and laughed again. "Let me spell it out for you, sweetie. It's. Not. Your. Baby." She smiled a tight little smile that didn't reach her eyes and held out her hands palms up, silently presenting her confession for me to digest.

"Not – " I repeated. She pursed her lips, raising her eyebrows, waiting for the penny to drop. "Christopher. It's his."

She broke into a slow clap that tore at my insides. She must know how hard this was to hear, how her revelation would destroy me, and yet there was no sense of apology or embarrassment on her part. I could see exactly what she was feeling by the flash in her eyes, the little flushed patches that bloomed on her cheekbones. She was angry. With me. For making her have to talk about something she clearly considered done and dusted.

"Exactly, genius," she said coldly. "So you can give up your sickly sweet fantasy about playing happy families, because it's not your baby."

"Does he know?" I asked quietly.

She shook her head. "Do we really need to discuss this any further?"

"Yes. We do."

Rolling her eyes, she shrugged as if every word wasn't tearing out my heart. She picked up a bottle of gin from the side and poured a generous measure into a glass, knocking it back in one go. I blinked, shocked at her disregard for the baby. "No, Joshua," she said, turning to look at me. "I haven't informed the father of my child." I recoiled, her words wounding like a knife twisting in my gut. "And I won't. What would be the point? Besides, I don't have his number. I told you, it was a one off. It wasn't like we stayed in touch," she said, as if she expected me to praise her for that.

"So what now?" I asked. I didn't know how I was supposed to react. It wasn't as if her night with Christopher had been a secret. She'd told me as soon as it had happened and I'd forgiven her. But I hadn't bargained for a pregnancy. A *baby*.

"I told you," she sighed. "I'll get rid of it and we'll forget the whole mess ever happened. I only told you because they said you'll need to drive me home. Oh, and I might need looking after. I'll be sore, you know?"

I didn't understand how she could be so flippant. So cold. This was a baby, and what did it matter if it was created by me or some other guy? Did that mean we shouldn't even discuss it? That it had to be doomed from the start?

"Keep it," I said softly. "We can do this, Fran. We can be a family."

"I didn't peg you for the type of man who would

tell a woman what to do with her own body!" she spat. "It's not your choice. Do you get that? It's up to me!"

"I know that. And I'd never try to force you to have the baby if you really didn't want to. I'm not saying you can't choose. But you haven't even considered keeping it. You assumed I'd be angry. That I'd want it brushed under the carpet. I'm telling you, I'm not. I *want* kids. I do. I want to be a dad."

"But you won't be a dad! You'll be the guy who has to take care of the cuckoo child. I'm telling you, Joshua, you'll resent me and *it* from the moment the thing is born. It will be a constant reminder of what I did."

"No, it won't be like that."

"It's not yours, Josh."

I stared at her. "It *could* be. If we got married, it could be mine. Nobody need know any different. You put my name on the birth certificate, the baby takes my last name. It wouldn't matter that I didn't provide the sperm. He'd be mine."

She stared back, her face a picture of confusion.

"Are you serious? You're asking me to marry you?"

I glanced at the door, realising that I was suddenly faced with the biggest crossroads of my life. I could take the easy path, tell her I couldn't forgive her this. That I knew she couldn't change and the pain had outweighed the good in our relationship. Part of me wanted to do it, now that it was laid out in front of me. I could justify leaving. Nobody would blame me. I wouldn't even have to admit the rest of it. The person she became when she didn't get her own way, the things she was capable of when I caught her in the wrong mood. Nobody need know the whole truth. Just this small part. I could be free of her.

Or I could traipse up the difficult path. The one that was sure to have plenty of obstacles and challenges along the winding route. The one I may not survive. It was no doubt harder, less simple, but it was the path a real man would take. The one that didn't leave a pregnant woman alone to cope, whether she kept the baby or not. If I pushed forward, I would have a chance at having the happy family I'd always dreamed of. Mummy, daddy and baby all under one roof, nothing like the stark, cruel home I'd been raised in. It wouldn't be perfect, and it would take a hell of a lot of hard work, but as my mother used to tell me, nothing worth having is ever easy.

I cleared my throat making my decision, my heart thumping in my chest. My palms were suddenly dripping with sweat and I wiped them on my jeans, dropping down onto one knee. For a second, I had the strongest urge to get up and run. I swallowed it down and smiled up at her, pushing down my fear and the feeling in my belly which was screaming at me to reconsider. "Yes, Franchesca. I'm serious. Will you marry me?"

Chapter Twenty-Two

Josh

So it was done. I was officially a married man. I glanced across the dance-floor, catching Franchesca's eye and she smiled widely at me, her eyes sparkling with the excitement of the day. Her dress was cut cleverly to minimise her growing stomach, but even so, it was obvious she was carrying precious cargo within her womb. Her face, usually slim and delicate, was now round and carried the rosy flush of the third trimester. The morning sickness had long since passed and we were approaching the final weeks. I couldn't wait to meet my child. I already knew it was a boy. I'd hardly been able to stop myself from bursting into happy tears at the ultrasound appointment.

Franchesca blew me a kiss across the room and turned from me, her attention caught by a pair of chattering aunts who's names I'd forgotten. Her mother was somewhere in the vicinity, and though I'd tried to arrange it more times than I could count, today had been our first meeting. When she'd made her way into the hall after the ceremony, coming to shake my hand, I'd been surprised to discover a woman who mirrored Fran in nearly every regard. She had the same petite yet curvy figure, glossy, dark hair and full lips, and on top of that, she clearly shared the same intimidating intelligence as her daughter.

I already knew she was a physicist and that Fran had followed in her footsteps by going into science, but I'd expected – and hoped – to see a modicum of affection between the two of them. A mother was supposed to be emotional and sentimental on her only daughter's wedding day, wasn't she? But there had been no tears, no hugs or teasing about her choice to wear white. No mention of how her late father would have been proud to walk her down the aisle. It was like witnessing an awkward interaction between rival colleagues rather than a long awaited family reunion. Vanessa had held out a stiff hand for me to shake, given a brisk nod of congratulations to the pair of us, and moved on without bothering to make small talk.

I found it very strange that she hadn't bothered to

ask me anything about myself, nor pay Fran a single compliment, but then, who was I to judge? I'd invited no family whatsoever. I was grateful of the excuse that my mother was dead and buried. I wouldn't have known how to cope if she'd been at my wedding. Not that I'd have ever made it this far with Fran if *she* was in the picture. She'd maintained her rigid control over every aspect of my life right up until the day she'd died, and I'd felt nothing but relief on the day of her funeral. The thought of her face, her *voice* still had the power to make my bowel contract painfully, my mouth dry and my hands damp with the fear her memory still conjured up within me. Never having known my father, I couldn't invite him, and any other family would have been nothing more than a stranger to me. I had no need for them. I'd made my own family. My friends and teammates and now my wife and soon to be son.

Brett approached, loosening his tie and smiling widely. He wrapped me in a tight hug, slapping me on the back enthusiastically. "You did good, mate. Didn't let yourself down."

"Thanks for not losing the rings," I teased, pulling back to grin at him.

"Thanks for trusting me with them. Honestly, Josh, it was an honour." He sat down at one of the small round tables dotted around the beautifully decorated room and I followed suit. "So," he said, leaning towards me. "Married. We've come a bloody long way, you and me."

I nodded. "You'll be next."

"You may well be right. Millie's been weird today. Wedding fever, I think. You've been putting ideas in her head."

"But you'll propose? I mean, it's going well?"

"It is. Better than I could have imagined. But we're in no rush."

"Speak for yourself," I grinned, nodding my head towards the bar. Brett followed my gaze to where Millie stood holding Franchesca's bouquet and smiling like a Cheshire cat.

"Damn." He leaned back in his chair and looked at me quizzically. "I can't pretend I wasn't surprised when you told me you were getting married though," he said, catching me off guard. "I mean, I always got the impression that you two..."

"What?" I asked, going suddenly cold.

"I don't know. It's nothing really. But there have been times when I half expected you to call it off. You haven't always seemed happy, you know?"

I stared at him, bile rising in my throat. I'd always gone to so much effort to hide our issues, Fran's mood-swings, from the outside world. I never told anyone the things she said and did behind closed doors because it was none of their business. It would have been humiliating to admit. The idea that Brett, and who knew who else, had seen even a glimpse of our troubles had my stomach churning with fear. With as much effort as I could muster, I gave a casual shrug. "We've had our spats. Every relationship does, nothing's always smooth sailing, is it? But no, mate, we're happy. I wouldn't have asked her to marry me if we weren't."

"Are you sure? I mean, you know you can always talk to me, right?" he coughed, clearly embarrassed at making the offer. But he didn't look away or make a joke and that made it all the more humiliating for me. I had no idea what it was he'd seen that made him worry, but if Brett was making the effort to have such a deep heart to heart with me, it was obvious that our relationship issues hadn't been as private as I thought.

"Thanks for that, mate," I grinned, getting to my feet. "But you're not getting the details of the wedding night."

"Your wife's eight months pregnant. I think your wedding night will involve foot massages and finding the heartburn medicine," he laughed, rising to his feet. His smile faded and he frowned, clapping me on the shoulder and pursing his lips thoughtfully. I had the awful sense he was about to get serious again.

"Come on, we're letting a free bar go to waste. Let's get a beer," I said, flashing him a reassuring grin. I turned before he had chance to object and strode across the dance-floor, not letting my smile slide even for a second.

It was past one a.m. when the guests finally started leaving. Fran and I stood at the door, accepting hugs and well wishes from hoards of merry friends and family. Mike shuffled along the line, leaning in to kiss Fran's cheek and shake my hand, and his wife, Lara stopped to compliment Fran on her dress and pat her bump. I watched surreptitiously, hoping the innocent action hadn't annoyed my wife. She hated to be reminded of her changing figure, but Lara was such a sweetheart. She couldn't know how sensitive Fran was about it. Lara stepped towards me, wrapping her arms around my neck and kissing my cheek exuberantly. "It's so wonderful to see you finally settled, Josh. It's been a lovely day. You make a beautiful couple."

"Thank you, Lara," I grinned as she pulled back.

Mike wrapped an arm around her waist. "Come on, sweetheart. Let's get you home. Got to make the most of the babysitter," he winked over her head. She pushed him playfully and I watched them leave, hoping Fran and I would get to where they were someday. They had the healthiest marriage I'd ever seen and I looked up to both of them almost as if they were parents to me, though they weren't nearly old enough to be.

The rest of the guests left and finally Fran and I were alone, with only the waiters and bar-staff for company. "Shall we go up to the honeymoon suite, Mrs. Jones?" I said, offering my arm. She took it silently and we walked slowly through the hall, making our way through the maze of corridors and up several richly carpeted staircases. There was a tension in the air between us and I hoped it was nothing but tiredness on her part. It had been a long, emotional day and she was heavily pregnant. I expected she just needed a lie down and some peace and quiet. I smothered a grin, remembering Brett's prediction for my less than sensual wedding night. The bastard had been right.

I slid the key in the door, pushed it open and turned to carry her over the threshold, but she walked past me without waiting. Probably for the best. I would have hated to make her or the baby uncomfortable. I stepped inside, pushing the door closed behind me, moving to take off my tie. She reached forward as if she were going to help me and I smiled down at her as she loosened it, taking in how beautiful she looked in her dress. She was glowing, like an angel. It was a memory I would keep forever, but as I looked at her face, I realised she wasn't smiling. She had a look in her eye which I knew only too well, and all at once, before she'd even yanked the thick material of my tie around my windpipe, I knew what was coming.

She glared up at me, squeezing the tie tight around my throat and I grasped at the material, pulling it away, gasping for air. I stumbled back against the door and she launched herself at me, punching and scratching and yanking at my hair, my ears. I felt the familiar sting of her fingernails ripping through my cheek, her knee colliding with my crotch and I fell to my knees, breathless. She stepped back, her nostrils flaring and cast around her, looking for something. I couldn't even speak. I couldn't believe she would choose tonight of all nights to give into her anger and taint the first night of our marriage with her venom.

I wanted to crawl away from her, to be

somewhere dark and alone where I could cry and mourn the wedding night that we would never have now. She'd ruined it. I was aware of movement and then she was back again, her hand grabbing a fistful of my short hair, yanking my face up to meet hers. There was no love in her eyes. No doubt. She lifted something high in the air and I realised she was holding my new phone, the upgraded model to my old android. Without hesitating, she brought it down, colliding hard against my cheekbone. I fell sideways, my hands forming a cage around my head, afraid to put them out and stop her for fear that I would catch the baby. It would only make her more angry anyway. She was so much like my mother.

She hit me with the phone a second time and then a third, and I felt the swelling bruise bloom across my cheek, the pain shooting through my temple as she laid into me with her full strength. She stood, breathless then with a scream of rage, she threw the phone across the room. It hit the wall and I heard her sigh with satisfaction as she went to retrieve it. A cobweb of cracks ran from top to bottom blemishing the once pristine screen.

I knew the rules of this game. I was supposed to ask. To beg for an explanation for my punishment, to apologise for causing her to lose her cool. It was what she was waiting for. I knew it. But I couldn't bring myself to speak. For the first time since we'd met, I felt something I didn't know I had in me. I was frightened. I was hurt and bleeding and terrified that she would hit me again. I knew I wouldn't be able to fight back. I would never be able to do that. But along with my fear, there was also a simmering fury that she'd chosen to do this tonight of all nights. She had ruined something that should have been sacred, and I didn't think I could ever forgive her for that.

I didn't make any move to get up from my position on the floor at the edge of the bed, nor to speak. I stayed on my side, my eyes open, waiting for the next blow. A sudden knock echoed through the room and both of us jumped. Fran took a breath and walked slowly to the door. She opened it wide so it hit me in the back of the head and I gasped, then bit the inside of my cheek so as not to make a sound.

"I am so sorry to disturb you, madam," came a worried male voice. "I would never normally dream of doing so, but a disturbance was heard and I wanted to check you and Mr. Jones were alright?"

"Oh, I'm sorry," Franchesca gushed in her sweetest voice. "We're quite alright. I think my husband had a little too much to drink and he fell over. Knocked over the side table and it made quite a noise, I'm afraid. Please apologise to the other guests for us, I'll make sure it doesn't happen again," she said, her voice husky and sensual.

"Oh, right," the voice came again, and I could picture his flushed face. I knew the impact Fran had on men when she wanted to win them over. He was no doubt blushing. "Would you like me to send someone in to clean up?"

"No, thank you. We'll be fine." I saw her fingers move to unbutton her dress, her eyes still sultry as she stared at at the unseen visitor.

"Okay, right, well if you need anything, don't hesitate to call down to reception."

"I won't." She smiled and shut the door softly,

turning to look at me. Without a word, she stepped out of the hefty dress and stood in her cream corset and stockings, still wearing her shoes. She stepped forward her heel coming to rest on my open palm. "Shhhhh," she said, holding a finger to her lips as I writhed in pain.

I tried to pull away but she pushed down harder. "You're not to see that woman again, do you understand me?" she said softly. I didn't answer. I couldn't, I had no idea what she was talking about and the pain was all I could concentrate on. She eased her foot back and I sighed in relief. "Lara. Pretty little Lara. Quite the figure she's got, hasn't she?"

"What? I - "

Her heel pushed down again and I groaned, instinctively reaching out for her ankle. "Uh, uh, uh," she said, waggling a finger as if she were telling a child not to dip into the biscuit tin for a second cookie. "Wouldn't want me to trip and land on your precious baby, would you darling?" she pushed her heel deeper and I felt the skin split open, a white hot pain spreading like fire through my hand.

"Condescending bitch, patting me on the stomach like some prize fucking heifer then throwing herself over *my* husband. I bet you two have had more than a few illicit kisses behind Mike's back, haven't you? I saw how she looked at you! How many times have you slept with her, huh, Josh?"

"Fran, please stop!"

"Say you won't see her again!"

"I can't, Fran, she's like family to me, her and Mike are like parents to me, you know that!"

"I know that's the tidy little story you put out into the world. But it isn't the truth, is it? You're jealous of Mike. You want what he's got. You told me before."

"I meant a marriage like his. A happy home. Not his *wife*. I just meant that I want *us* to be as close as they are, for Christ sake!"

"I don't believe you. I don't believe a word you say. How can I when you let women touch you like that when I'm right next to you? What must you let them do when I'm not around? I know what men are like, you're no different!"

"Are you serious! You're the only one of us who's

cheated! You're the one carrying another man's child!"

"And you forgave me for that a little too easily, didn't you? I always wondered why. But it's obvious when you think about it. You could hardly fly off the handle when you were sneaking around with Lara, could you?"

"You're fucking insane!"

"No, Josh, I'm your wife. Your *pregnant* wife. And I won't put up with your shit anymore, okay? I don't want you messaging and scrolling through other women's photos online. I won't have you disrespect me."

"I have no idea what you mean," I said, unable to hold back the tears now. "I've done nothing wrong." She lifted her heel ever so slightly, and I took my opportunity, pulling my hand from beneath it, feeling the broken skin tearing as I yanked it away from her. I pulled it close to my chest and curled into a tight ball, waiting for the next blow. She laughed coldly.

"Everyone thinks you're such a hero, don't they, Josh? If only they could see you now, they would all know you're a weak, pathetic loser. If only your precious Mike and Lara knew the truth. Maybe I'll show them someday."

She picked up her own phone from the bedside cabinet, and I heard the click as she snapped a photo of me. "Say cheese, loser," she smiled. She shook her head then walked to the en-suite. "I'm going for a bath. This baby is hurting my back. Clear up this mess, will you?" She didn't wait for an answer as she slammed the door closed.

Chapter Twenty-Three

Josh

What the hell is that thing you're carrying around?" Brett yelled, dropping his spoon clumsily into his half eaten bowl of cereal and getting up from the table. He strode towards me his hand outstretched.

"It's a phone. I'm pretty sure you've seen one before," I said, trying to shove the brick sized thing back into my pocket. Brett lurched forward, grabbing it from my hands, turning it one way and then another with a sneer spread across his face. "It's a relic. An antique." He pressed a few buttons and frowned. "No internet, no camera, no *anything*. Where's your *real* phone?"

"It broke."

"So... get a new one? You aren't so underpaid you have to put up with this thing, are you?"

I tried to shrug nonchalantly, but I could feel the tension stretched across my cheekbones. "I will, but I've not had time to go and pick one up. I had this old one in the drawer and it's better than nothing." I didn't want to tell him I'd already replaced my old phone. I'd ordered a new one the day after the wedding, hoping that Franchesca would choose to keep quiet. Sometimes, after she lashed out so dramatically, she had a sense of shame about her. She went with the *let's pretend it never happened* approach, and I had hoped that she'd take that route this time.

Only, she hadn't been ready to drop it. Not at all. Maybe I'd made my move too soon. I never even saw what happened to the new android I'd had delivered. All I knew was that we went to bed, the tense silence filling the spaces between our rigid bodies, as we lay as far apart as possible on the queen sized mattress. The new phone had been charging on the dresser in our room, having only arrived that afternoon. And when I woke up in the morning, it was gone, this nineties relic in its place.

I knew I should confront her. Demand my new phone back, the phone I'd paid for out of my own money, that I'd only had to buy because *she'd* lost control. But I hadn't been able to summon the courage. I hadn't known how to get the words out without crumbling. So I'd picked up the ugly, barely functional joke of a phone, and without a word to my wife, I'd shoved the thing in my pocket and pretended everything was fine.

Brett clasped a rough hand on my shoulder, his face peering into mine, his eyes twinkling with playful sarcasm. "You know you can order them online, right? Takes two minutes and you can get next day delivery. How are you supposed to do anything with this thing?" he said, shaking his head as he bashed the clunky buttons. The screen wasn't even in colour. "No wonder you've been so shit at replying to my Facebook messages. Are you even bothering to check them on the computer?"

"Messages? What messages?"

"Me and Mills' invited you guys round for dinner last week, but never got a reply. And then there was bowling for Rebecca's birthday on Sunday. I thought you were too loved up in your newly-wedded bliss to bother to reply, but now I've seen the state of your tech, maybe *this* is the reason."

"Yeah, maybe." I looked down at the phone, pretending to be preoccupied with it. I'd seen no messages. The truth was, I hadn't been online in weeks. The phone had been only the beginning of my troubles, as it turned out. It had been less than three days after the wedding, when Franchesca had flown off the handle and begun laying down her new rules. She'd demanded access to all my social media accounts, then changed the passwords herself, warning me not to go behind her back and try to reset them.

She'd made me stand over her, watching as she read each and every one of my messages and emails, even writing replies to a few, signing off with my name. The playful tone I'd always had in my conversations with Rebecca, and the open warmth I had with Lara had been like a red flag to a bull. Fran had been furious for days having read their emails. She couldn't understand why Lara would finish messages with *Love Lara* if we weren't going behind her back. As hard as I tried, I couldn't get her to calm down and see that it was purely platonic, nothing sinister or deceitful.

I'd been stuck indoors, my face still swollen and bruised from the wedding night, my body aching from head to toe. I knew I had to talk to her about what she'd done, but every time I tried, my resolve shattered and I found myself biting my trembling lip, unable to force out the questions I knew she couldn't answer.

"Here," Brett said, breaking into my thoughts. He held up his own phone to show me the picture of the smartphone on the screen. "This one's on sale until tomorrow. Order it now and we'll keep the piss taking to a minimum. I can't allow you to walk around with that monstrosity clamped to your ear," he said, his eyes sparkling. "Not if you want to be seen with someone as cool as me."

I felt a sudden urge to cry. I knew he was only teasing. That it was all in jest. He wasn't about to rip the thing from my hands and smash it to pieces in front of me. He couldn't care less if I was 'cool' or not. He was just having a bit of fun, winding me up. Not like my wife. The woman who was supposed to love me, but who hurt me more than anybody else.

I had the sudden urge to tell him everything. To let him in on my dirty little secret. The sham that was my life, my relationship. I wanted, more than anything, for him to hear the truth and tell me what to do, because I was beyond lost and confused. I didn't know how to make Franchesca happy. To stop her from descending into these vicious attacks on me. If I could help her, we could be the kind of couple I'd always dreamed of being a part of. I knew we could. We had good times. But more and more they were becoming spoiled by her need to control me, to make me bow to her every demand. Just like it had been with my mother.

I wanted to ask for help more than anything. But I couldn't. It was too shameful, too humiliating. And good a friend as he was, he could never understand why I'd let it go so far. How a man of my size could let himself be cowed by an eight stone woman. Because that was the truth. She dominated me. Ruled me. And I could see no escape. She would never let me leave. The thought shocked me. For the first time since I'd discovered she was pregnant, I wished that I'd had the sense to walk away the moment I found out. To take the opportunity and run before it was too late.

The alarm sounded shrilly through the fire-station and I swallowed down my sadness, running towards the engine, towards the only thing I knew I was capable of. As I climbed into the driver's seat, a little thought popped into my mind. How long until she tries to take this from me?

Chapter Twenty-Four

Josh

Everything was so familiar, yet so wrong. The siren blasting around us was too fast, too high pitched, I was sitting in the back, rather than my usual position up front and worst of all, the emergency wasn't in some distant street we were rushing towards. It was here, now, happening right in front of me.

I hadn't expected to meet my child in the back of an ambulance, but it was looking increasingly likely from the sounds Franchesca was currently emitting, and the strength of her shaking hand clenched around mine. I leaned towards the blur of the tinted window, trying to figure out where we were, how far we had to go, but in the darkness of the night with the street-lamps streaking past us, it was impossible to tell.

I should have known. When I'd arrived back from my shift, Franchesca had seemed different from usual. Soft. Vulnerable even. She'd snuggled into my chest and told me she'd been missing me all day. When I asked why she'd been at home, rather than at work, she'd shrugged and said she'd felt achy, her stomach was heavy, so she'd decided to catch up on some paperwork from the comfort of the sofa. There were only a few weeks left until her due date, and she was really beginning to struggle with the lack of energy and the increasing aches and pains.

I'd spent the evening coaxing her to eat the dinner I'd made and rubbing her lower back, then we'd cuddled up together in contentment on the sofa. I loved when she was soft and loving like this. I could be the strong one, the protector, and I knew she wasn't about to snap. She never did on these rare occasions. I wished it could always be so simple.

We'd gone to bed, only for her to get back up twenty minutes later, complaining about the baby pushing on her bladder. When she hadn't returned, I'd got up to go and find her. I'd laughed when I found her squatting down on the bathroom floor, holding the edge of the bath for support, thinking she was trying out some yoga stretch or something. But when she looked up at me, the smile disappeared instantly from my face and I knew it was time. She'd never looked at me like that. Like she was scared. Uncertain. It was nice to know she had it in her, even if this was the one and only time she'd let it out.

I'd thought we would have loads of time. We'd monitor the contractions, get her bag together and drive to the maternity unit. That had been the plan. But when I tried to help her up, she shook her head and whispered the words that sent everything into chaos. "It's coming, Josh. It's coming now." All my training, my ability to stay calm in the face of emergency, seemed to disappear in a puff of smoke, and now, sitting in the back of the ambulance with only a single paramedic to support me, I knew we wouldn't make it to the hospital before she gave birth.

Fran dug her nails deep into the back of my hand, her eyes wild with fear. "I want an epidural! They said I could have one!"

"Not here," the paramedic said. "And not now. You're past the point of no return." He flashed a wide grin at me, and I shook my head in confusion. I couldn't see what he had to be so cheerful about.

"Do you know what you're doing?" I asked him, not caring that I sounded rude and ungrateful. I was filled with terror at the idea of all the things that could go wrong. What if the baby got stuck? What if Fran haemorrhaged? What if they both died?

He clapped a hand on my shoulder, flashing me a reassuring smile. "Her body knows exactly what to do. But yes, I've done this a thousand times before. She's in safe hands."

Fran gave an almighty bellow and arched her back, her eyes squeezed shut as her face turned almost purple with the strain of pushing. "And the head is out," the paramedic said, beaming around at us. Fran seemed not to hear him. She didn't even have time to open her eyes before she tensed with the pain of another contraction. "That's it, Franchesca, I'd say one last big push and it will all be done and dusted. Not too hard now, slowly does it, that's it, that's it... and... yes! Well done, you clever girl!"

I flinched at his patronising tone, sure that Fran would baulk at his words, but then, my attention was diverted by the soft, pink little baby, covered in thick white vernix, a gurgling wail filling the confined space in the back of the ambulance. The paramedic cut the cord, wrapping the tiny, wriggling thing in a blue cotton blanket, and held the little bundle towards Franchesca. "Congratulations. You have a little boy." He placed the baby in her arms and I squeezed my lips tightly together, trying to keep my emotions under control as I watched them.

Fran peered down at the baby, a frown puckering her forehead. "It's over..." she murmured.

I bent low to look at him over her shoulder. "He's perfect, Fran, absolutely perfect. You were incredible," I said, reaching down to sweep the sweat matted hair back from her face, waiting to see the inevitable flood of love fill her face. The rush of endorphins as she held the child she'd carried within her own body all these months. Instead, she stared up at me, her expression devoid of anything resembling emotion.

"We'll call him Edwin. After my grandfather."

"Edwin..." I repeated, rolling the name over my tongue. I didn't like it. It was an old fashioned name that would no doubt lead to him being bullied when he reached school age.

"Edwin Jones," she said, watching my face closely.

"Oh," I breathed. I hadn't dared to ask about the last name. When we'd agreed to get married, we'd said he would take my name, but I hadn't quite believed she would let me have such a gift. It made him mine. Truly mine, despite what his biology might say.

"Here. You take him." She held out her arms and I lurched forward, fearful that she would drop him. I let his tiny body sink into my arms, cradling him close against my chest. He had a tiny tuft of fluffy blonde hair on top of his head and his eyes were wide as he stared up at me, dark and alert.

"Hello, little one," I said softly, sliding my finger into his palm, smiling as he gripped it tightly.

"Oh, you're going to be a great daddy, I can tell," the paramedic said, poised ready at the end of the narrow stretcher, as he waited for the placenta. I raised my eyes to thank him, and realised that Fran had rolled on her side, turning her back on us. "Oh, nothing to worry about," he said in a stage whisper, following my gaze. "She's just tired. Takes a lot out of you, this birth business. Enjoy those cuddles while you can, I doubt you'll get a look in once she's back on her feet. Nothing like the bond between a mother and son."

An image of my own mother snarling down on me, as I cowered against the wall in our run down council house flashed before my eyes, and I held Edwin a little tighter, hoping Fran would never dare to treat our son the way she treated me. I would stand for a lot of things from her, but never that. Not even if it killed me to stand up to her. I would never let her touch our child in anger. I realised I was shaking at the thought of it and swallowed thickly, nodding my agreement. "You're right," I managed. "I'm sure she's just a bit tired."

Chapter Twenty-Five

Josh

"Oh for Christ sake, this bloody child just wants, wants, wants!" Franchesca's voice echoed through the house.

I ran up the stairs taking them two at a time, rushing into the nursery. I'd tried to get her to bring him in with us, but she wouldn't have it, telling me she wanted to get him settled in his own space right from the start. She insisted that she didn't want to create any bad habits, though I didn't see how having his bassinet in our room could be considered a bad habit. It wasn't like he only needed someone to take care of him during the hours of daylight.

Fran was standing over the changing table, stripping the wet nappy off the screaming baby with less than gentle hands. I rushed forward, reaching out to stroke his forehead to calm his frantic cries. Fran glared at me. "Would it kill you to do a fucking nappy every now and then, Mr. Fucking Perfect?"

I bit my tongue at the ridiculousness of her

accusation. In the ten days since Edwin had been born, I had taken on ninety-five percent of his care, from nappies to feeds. Fran had shunned the very suggestion of breastfeeding outright, saying there was no point getting him reliant on her when she had every intention of going back to work.

As for night feeds, there had never been any question that it would be me who got up from the warm bed to go and sit with him, cuddling up with a bottle in the nursery. I was exhausted, the living embodiment of the new mother, but Fran was the one acting like the minimal disruption to her sleep was the end of the world. She stuck the tabs down on the nappy, not bothering to put his baby-grow back on, then handed him to me without a word.

"We're going out this afternoon," she said, making for the door.

"We are? Where?"

"We've got two visits at local nurseries, and then I'm interviewing a nanny on Thursday. I haven't decided which type of care would be best for us yet."

I ran my fingers through my hair, trying to keep

up with the conversation. My eyes itched with exhaustion and the realisation that I wouldn't be able to join Eddie for his nap made my heart sink. Bedtime seemed a long way off. "There's no rush, is there? We've got months to sort all this stuff out. Why stress over it now?"

"Months? What are you talking about?"

"Before you go back to work, I mean. You said you had a minimum of nine months. Although, I was thinking, you should probably take the full year. It's silly not to when your company offer such a great maternity package," I said, adjusting the baby into an upright position so he could see the view from the window over my shoulder.

She made a little noise in the back of her throat and held up her hand towards me, palm first. "Excuse me, what was that? Take a *year* off work? A *year*? Are you insane! Why the hell would I do that?"

"Because it's good for little Eddie, sorry," I flinched, realising my mistake. "Edwin. It's good for Edwin to be with you. I mean, how long were you planning to take?"

She threw back her head and laughed, gripping the door-frame for support. When she looked back at me, her eyes were glittering as if I'd made some hilarious joke. "Joshua, you simple minded little man. I'm not throwing away the career I've worked my arse off for, so that I can stay home and play peekaboo. I'm going back at the beginning of next month."

"What? You can't be serious. He'll be barely three weeks old. You can't want to palm him off on strangers!"

"Oh, everyone does these days. He'll be fine. And we'll all be happier if we're not crowding into each other's space. He wants something *every* minute of the day. I'm not cut out for it, Josh. I can't stand it. The monotony, the lack of stimulation." She gave a shrug. "It's not up for discussion, I'm going back, so you can either come with me to see these nurseries, or I'll pick one myself."

"Fran, no. You *can't*. Just look at him. Look how tiny he is! You can't do this."

"Oh, but you can, right? I knew you were old fashioned, but this is taking it too far. Your two weeks paternity are nearly up! You get to leave! What did you think, huh? You could go back to your normal life and still have a pretty little wife at home, cooking you a pie from scratch and taking care of the baby, while you get to escape the drudgery of *this* for hours at a time? Was that what you planned, Josh? Do you think that's fair?"

"That's not what I – "

She held up her hand again, her lips pursed in a tight, angry line. "It's not a discussion. I've made up my mind. I'm not going to give up my life for a baby I didn't even want," she said, turning to leave.

"Don't you dare say that!"

She spun, glaring at me and I felt the fear swell in my belly. "Don't test me, Joshua. Don't even think of it."

She turned to leave the room, but I couldn't let her go. *"I'll* do it," I blurted out. "I'll apply for shared parental leave. I'm sure I'll be eligible if you're not taking maternity. I won't get paid much, nothing like the package your company was offering, but we'll manage."

227

"You'll give up work? Stay home with the baby?" she asked. She tried to hide her satisfaction but I could see it written all over her face.

I suddenly knew I was walking straight into a trap. She'd never hidden the fact that she thought herself so much smarter than me, but I wasn't so stupid I couldn't see what she'd done. She'd wanted this outcome from the start. Wanted me away from the job I loved, the one thing I'd refused to give up for her.

Even so, I didn't dare to call her bluff. I couldn't bear to see her put our son in the hands of people who wouldn't love him, where he'd just be another face, another invoice at the end of the month. I had no choice and she knew it.

I'd have to figure something out before the paternity leave was up, because I couldn't leave my job permanently. Not if I wanted to retain a shred of my independence. She already held the strings on so much of my life, I couldn't let her control me financially too.

"I'm not having our baby be dumped with a

bunch of strangers," I said. "If you won't take care of him, *I* will."

"Be my guest, darling," she smirked. "He's all yours."

Chapter Twenty-Six

Josh

"So, how are you finding being the modern man?" Mike chuckled down the phone. I tucked it under my chin, guiding the warm bottle to Eddie's expectant little mouth as I leaned back against the arm of the sofa. I could hear the murmur of voices in the background of the call, and smiled as I pictured Brett and Rebecca throwing grapes into each other's mouths, and all the usual antics I was missing in my absence. I didn't mind.

"Actually, I'm really loving it," I admitted, watching the contented expression cross Eddie's face as he began to drink. "I won't lie, I miss that thing I used to do... what was it called?"

"Uh, sleep?" Mike offered helpfully.

"That's the one. I'm so tired I'm seeing spots most of the time, but it's a small price to pay. He's smiling now, you know? He literally lights up when I come into the room. There's no feeling like it."

Mike laughed. "Well, if it's what works for you,

fair play. I know *I* couldn't do it."

"You *do* do it!"

"Not full time. I think I'd lose the plot if I didn't get to escape to work," he laughed. "Speaking of the joys of work, how's Fran coping with being back?"

I stared out of the window, wondering how to answer. There had been an unexpected side effect to her getting her way with the childcare situation. She had no qualms about leaving us first thing every morning, having banished me from her bedroom so I didn't disturb her precious sleep with my "constantly getting up for the baby!" Eddie and I were quite happy sleeping in the spare room, without her tutting and glaring in our direction every time he needed to be fed or burped. She'd gone off that first morning without so much as a kiss for the baby. It was hard for me to even comprehend her complete lack of conflict at leaving her newborn child. It was clear that she wasn't cut out for motherhood, though I'd pinned all my hopes on the baby bringing out her nurturing side. She was far happier slotting back into her old routines as if nothing had changed.

However, she was far from content. In the few weeks since she'd gone back, I'd noticed her mood take a frightening dive in the evenings. She would come home to find me settling Eddie down in his cot for the night, or giving him his bath, and rather than rush to join us, she would snap at me, then give me the silent treatment, acting as if I'd done something to offend her. It had taken almost a week for me to realise the issue. She was jealous. Jealous of the time and attention I was giving to our baby. Not because she wished it was her holding him, bathing him, feeding him. No. It was simply down to the fact that she had never been able to cope with sharing my attentions. It was horrifying to realise, but impossible to deny. She was threatened by the new, tiny person who had come onto our home and I had no idea how to get her to see the madness in that.

"Oh, she's doing fine," I murmured into the telephone as Mike cleared his throat expectantly. "Missing Eddie, of course, but she's not the *stay at home mother* type."

"No. I must admit, I could never picture it."

"What do you mean?"

"Oh, no offence intended, mate. Not all women are into it, are they? I mean, Lara was born to do it. She lights up at the little things the kids do, the flowers they pick for her, the scribbled drawings they give her. Some nights I have to tear her away from reading them the tenth bedtime story in a row, so that I can actually spend some time with her."

I nodded silently, instantly able to picture the scene. Lara radiated softness. When you spoke to her, there was never any doubt that she was listening fully, completely invested in whatever it was you happened to be saying. She was the kind of mother I'd hoped Franchesca would magically become when she saw our baby. But it wasn't to be.

Mike was still speaking, clearly conscious that he'd dug himself a hole he couldn't escape from. "I mean, these days, it's all interchangeable, isn't it? There isn't any such thing as pink and blue jobs anymore, and why should there be? If you want to take the leave with the baby, why the hell shouldn't you?" he coughed. "But, you *are* planning to come back, aren't you? When the paternity leave is up?"

I stared down at the baby who was slowly drifting to sleep in my arms. "Yeah," I said, knowing already how difficult it was going to be. The thought of leaving him made me sick to my stomach, but I couldn't walk away from my career. I couldn't give up my only thread of independence. I would really be trapped then. "I'm coming back. Don't you go replacing me, alright? I'll be back before you know it."

Chapter Twenty-Seven

Josh

Franchesca leaned forward, the strap of her dress slipping low on her shoulder as she picked up the bottle of Merlot from the coffee table, topping up my glass. She was in a rare good mood and I was determined not to spoil it, but I couldn't help but glance anxiously at the clock on the DVD player every few minutes. As the numbers moved closer towards eleven p.m. I felt myself grow more and more tense.

Eddie would be waking for his bottle any minute now, and though I knew it shouldn't, I was fully aware that the interruption to our evening would irritate Franchesca. She took a sip of her wine and placed her glass on the table, jazz music playing softly in the background. Why did we always end up listening to jazz? I *hated* jazz. I always had. But because Franchesca liked it, it was what we always had to have.

My exhaustion from getting up to Eddie night after night was taking a toll on my own mood. I could feel a mounting tension like a balloon swelling inside my chest with every interaction I had with Fran. Every time I had to apologise because the kitchen wasn't spotless, after taking care of the baby alone for the whole day. Every time I cooked something she didn't deem a high enough standard for her tastes. Her snarky reactions when her rants about her work colleagues were interrupted, as I ran to fetch our wailing son and bring up his wind. Even the dim glow of the baby monitor on the coffee table had managed to piss her off. I'd never found it difficult to apologise and fix the problem before. But her open irritation towards her own son had lit a match of protective anger inside me that I couldn't seem to extinguish.

She leaned forward now, kissing my neck, her intentions clear. "Hold on," I said, pulling back. I threw an apologetic glance at the baby monitor. "He'll be awake any second. I'll just pop up and give him a bottle, and then we won't have to worry about... interruptions," I said, the word tasting bitter in my mouth.

"Don't be ridiculous. He's fast asleep. No point in

disturbing him now." She moved closer, wrapping her arm around my neck. "Don't tell me you don't find me beautiful now that I've had a baby?"

"Of course I do. But – "

She silenced me with a kiss and I closed my eyes, weighing up the situation. If we were quick, we might be done before he woke, but she'd be angry if she thought I was hurrying my time with her. If I went to Eddie now, ignoring her protests, she'd be furious that I'd rejected her, because I knew that was exactly how she would see it. Whatever I did, I couldn't win. She yanked at my t-shirt, pulling it over my head, then kissed me again. The unmistakable sound of Eddie beginning to gurgle and stir sounded on the monitor.

"See?" I said, pulling back, arching around her to see the monitor. "He's waking. If I go now, I can be back to you in ten minutes."

"Leave it," she whispered, pulling the straps of her dress down her arms, letting the material drop to her waist. She unfastened her bra, tossing it on the carpet behind her, then lifted my hands, pressing them to her breasts. "I want your full attention, got it?" she said pursing her lips in a look she always used when she intended to be sexy. It had no affect on me. None whatsoever. All I could think of was Eddie lying there in the dark, waiting for me to come.

Fran bent low, kissing my neck again and my stomach tightened as the first rolling wail echoed around us. She pulled back and I sighed in relief, waiting for her to resign herself to the inevitable. Instead, she picked up the baby monitor and flicked the button on the side, switching it off. She placed it back on the table and smiled that coy little smile I'd grown to despise. "Now it's just us," she said, taking my hand and guiding it back to her bare skin.

I stared at her, open mouthed, my ears straining for the sound of Eddie's cries through the thick Victorian brickwork. I thought I might vomit. She was no better mother than she was a wife. I'd been an idiot to ever think she could change. She was damaged, broken somewhere deep inside and nothing could fix her selfish, narcissistic nature.

I moved on autopilot, my need to go to the baby overriding my fear of the woman who could turn in an instant. I lifted her from my lap, sliding her onto the sofa and stood up, walking purposefully towards the door.

"What are you doing?" she gasped.

"What the fuck do you think I'm doing? I'm going to our son! I'm doing the very thing *you* should be doing!"

"I told you to leave him! I'm sick of that baby, constantly in the way, demanding your attention until there's no room for anyone else! What about *me,* Josh? What about our relationship, or doesn't that matter to you now?"

I stopped in the doorway, shaking my head. "Can you hear yourself, Fran? You *disgust* me. You make me feel physically sick, do you realise that?"

"Joshua," she said, anger distorting her features. "If you dare choose him over me – " her fists curled tight against her sides but I didn't care. Not any more.

"I already have," I said. I didn't wait to hear her response as I sprinted from the room, heading for my son.

Chapter Twenty-Eight

Josh

The house was quiet as I stripped off Eddie's all-in-one PJs and wet nappy, dressing him again in a fresh clean outfit. My hands shook with exhaustion as I fiddled with the tiny poppers, trying to get them done up before Eddie became too hungry for his bottle to cooperate with me. I hadn't dared to go to sleep after rowing with Franchesca last night. I'd expected her to come for me. To dole out whatever punishment it was she saw fit for daring to stand up to her.

Every time my eyes had started to drift closed, I'd been jolted awake, thinking I could hear creaking floorboards, the slow squeak of the door hinge. I'd pushed her further than I'd ever dared and there would be a price to pay. I was certain of it. But I couldn't regret my actions, I'd had no choice.

I hoped Eddie would nap well today. I could catch up while Fran was out at work then be on my guard for tonight. The very fact that I had to do that made me swell with a new found anger I'd never experienced before. I'd been scared, cowed, humiliated and saddened by Fran over the course of our relationship, but never had I felt this all encompassing anger towards her. It was Eddie who'd ignited it, his arrival that had made me see the lie I'd been living laid bare before me.

When it was just the two of us, it was easy to make excuses for her. To look inwards to figure out what I'd said or done to stoke the fire of her fury. It was so simple to make it my fault. But Eddie was innocent. He could barely hold up his own head, let alone be the cause of so much malice. He made everything so crystal clear. The problem wasn't him, and it wasn't me. It was *her*.

Eddie kicked his legs and I smiled, picking him up from the mattress and lifting him to my shoulder. "Time for breakfast, little man," I said, heading out of the spare room and down the stairs, treading carefully. I'd held out till after seven thirty, not wanting to bump into Fran before she left for work. With any luck, she'd stay late and we could be back in bed before she even arrived home. Maybe I would pop out and get a lock for the spare-room door? If she was going to be extreme, why shouldn't I?

I made for the kitchen, filling the kettle with one hand, jiggling the baby to keep him calm.

"Give him to me."

I dropped the bottle I was holding on the counter and heard it bounce then hit the floor with a clatter, the creamy formula powder spilling over the tiles. I turned to see Franchesca standing in the kitchen doorway, staring at me with cold, hate filled eyes. She wore a white, wrap-around linen shirt and cropped pale blue trousers, her dark hair pulled back in a messy ponytail on top of her head.

"Fran, what are you still d-doing here? Shouldn't you be at w-work?" I stuttered, my arm tightening fractionally around the baby.

She held out her arms expectantly. "Yes, I should be. But it's apparent that you seem to think you can raise this child without boundaries, so here I am, rescuing you from your own incompetence. I've taken two weeks leave. *Unpaid* leave, she stressed. If you think I'm going to let this nonsense continue, you've got another thing coming."

"Nonsense? What are you talking about?"

She looked down at her fingernails, appraising the neat peach varnish, not bothering to meet my eyes as she replied. *"You. Him.* The fact that he only has to make the slightest whimper and you're running to serve him." She gave a tut and glared up at me again. "You're spoiling him, Joshua, you obviously haven't got a clue what you're doing, so *I'll* do it for you." She stepped forward, prizing Eddie from my arms. Instantly he started to cry. Fran gave another distinct tut as she looked down at his angry little face in disgust. "I knew I should have got a bloody nanny. You being super-dad was never going to work, was it?"

"We're doing fine. I know what I'm doing. He's doing great, Fran, can't you see that? I'm doing everything I should be."

"No, you're not." She didn't wait for me to respond. She span on her heel, heading for the stairs.

"Where are you taking him? He's not tired, he

needs *feeding,* Fran, he hasn't eaten yet," I said, following after her. She ignored me, heading back upstairs with a sense of purpose I found chilling. I paused at the bottom step, unsure how I could reason with her. I knew how impossible she could be when she set her mind to something. "I'll... I'll get his bottle ready," I muttered to myself, as she disappeared into the nursery.

I rushed back to the kitchen, scooping fresh formula haphazardly into a clean bottle, spilling half of it on the counter in my haste to get back to Eddie. If Fran was telling the truth about taking leave, the next two weeks would be hell for all three of us. Although, I thought, shaking the bottle hard, I couldn't picture it lasting. With anything else, she would be stubborn enough to see it through just to spite me, but baby care? I didn't think her resolve would last more than one sleepless night before she handed him back to me. I just had to stay calm and wait for her to come to that conclusion on her own. Her stubbornness to beat me would be outweighed by her inability to care for anyone other than herself.

Chapter Twenty-Nine

Josh

I paced back and forth on the landing outside Eddie's nursery, listening to the sounds of frantic crying coming from within. What could she be doing in there? How could the baby be so worked up with his mother right there beside him? It had been the longest, most painful six days of my life. Since that awful morning when Franchesca had demanded I hand Eddie over, she had refused to let me have anything to do with his care. She'd shut me out of rooms and stepped in-front of me every time I went to pick him up. He'd spent ninety percent of his time flat on his back in his cot, the curtains drawn to shut out any trace of sunlight in her misguided attempt to get him into a good sleep routine.

It was my punishment for going against her, and it hurt more than any physical injury she could have possibly thought up. I was going out of my mind, waiting for her to give in and say this ridiculous charade was over and I could have him back, but the more distressed I became, the more it fuelled her determination to keep going. My heart thumped hard against my ribcage, sweat prickling beneath my arms, the moisture evaporating from my mouth as I pictured him screaming behind the closed door. I made up my mind, straightened my back and took a deep breath, lunging forward to push open the door.

It took a moment to adjust to the half-light in the dim room, but then my eyes focused and I recoiled in shock. Fran was sitting in an armchair, her headphones secured firmly over her ears as she flicked casually through a magazine. She didn't even hear me come in. Eddie was lying on his back in his cot, his breath ragged between choking sobs. A pile of vomit pooled beside his tiny head, congealing in his downy hair, drying in his feathery eyelashes.

I rushed forward snatching him up into my arms, feeling as though I could vomit myself. My sudden movement caught Fran's eye and she yanked off her headphones, jumping to her feet. "Put him down right now! I told you to leave this to me!" she screamed, lurching forward. She made a grab for the baby but I stepped back. His tiny body coiled against my chest, trembling all over. I couldn't believe she could do this to her own child. Such a tiny helpless little being, reliant on her for his every need, and *still* she couldn't summon an ounce of compassion.

"This is too much, even from you, Fran," I said quietly, refusing to raise my voice to match hers. Eddie had been traumatised enough without hearing me shouting at his mother. "You aren't capable of taking care of a plant, let alone a baby. I won't let you do this to our child. He deserves better."

"I don't think that's your decision to make, is it?"

I stared at her, wondering how I could have ever thought she was the kind of woman I wanted. The answer to all my problems. There had been a time I would have forgiven her anything, but not now. All I could see was a cruel, selfish, heartless woman, who would go so far as to use a baby to get at me. "I'm leaving you," I said softly, my eyes on hers. I wanted her to know how certain I was in my decision. She would see no fear in my eyes. No chink in my armour. "I can't bear to spend another night under the same roof as you. I'm leaving. And I'm taking him with me."

She gave a cold laugh that echoed around the room, mingling with Eddie's diminishing whimpers. "Leave then. I'm bored of you anyway. But you aren't taking him."

I felt a fiery determination ignite in my belly, knowing what was at stake if I backed down, even a tiny bit. I gritted my teeth, breathing heavily. "Oh, I am. Do you think I'm insane? I wouldn't leave him with you for anything. You aren't capable of doing this, Fran. You're never going to be a mother in anything but name. Do you think because you gave birth to him, that makes you a parent? A real mum? No, Fran, it doesn't. It's the things you *do,* the sacrifices you're willing to make, and we both know, you aren't prepared to make a single one. You can't even bear to get out of bed to feed him. You're a joke, Fran, and we both know you don't want him. But *I* do. And I'm telling you, Eddie is coming with me."

I turned, heading for the door. "He's not yours,

Josh." She stepped forward, a tight smile on her lips. "Not your baby, not your problem." She gave a satisfied smirk and for the first time in my life, I felt the urge to hit her.

"My name's on the birth certificate. He's *my* son. And I'm taking him. I know why you're doing this, and it has nothing to do with wanting him, and everything to do with hurting me. You don't care as long as you win, do you? It's all just a twisted little game. But this is important. He needs a level of care you can't give him! What kind of life would he have with a mother like you?"

She moved in a split second, flying at me with her eyes wide, punching my cheekbone with as much force as she could muster, before cracking her fist into my nose. I stumbled back, my arms forming a cage around the baby, desperate not to let him slip from my grasp. Blood streamed into my mouth, dripping onto Eddie's face as he looked up at me. A drop fell onto his cheek and he screwed up his eyes, turning his face away.

I straightened, fixing Fran with a cold stare. I

knew what she expected. She wanted me to cower. To *beg*. But I wasn't going to do that now. I couldn't let her win. I took a breath, swallowing back my fear, refusing to let my eyes drop from hers as they always seemed to do. "And you expect me to leave a baby in your care? You disgust me."

She flinched, then shrugged away my words as if they didn't matter, reaching slowly into her pocket. Despite myself I felt terror bloom in my gut, wondering what she was about to pull out. I hoped, beyond anything, it wouldn't be a knife. I almost laughed when I saw the folded piece of paper. She held it up victoriously. "See this? It's a DNA test confirming that you aren't Edwin's natural father. It doesn't matter what the birth certificate says, Joshua. He *isn't* yours. So leave. *Go*. I don't fucking care. But you won't take the baby."

"Is that so?" I breathed. I grabbed the paper from her hand, screwing it into a ball and shoving it in my pocket without even bothering to glance at it. It meant nothing. As far as Eddie knew, *I* was his daddy. That was good enough for me. I walked from the room, my whole body trembling as I made for the stairs, my heart hammering so hard I could hear it in my ears, feel it in my throat. Franchesca ran after me, and I knew she wouldn't back down without a fight. I had to be strong, for Eddie's sake. I had to be the father he deserved, the kind of man I'd wished for my whole childhood, to step in and protect me from my mother's wrath.

I stepped onto the stairs, my arms wrapped tightly around the baby. "Joshua, give him to me! Now!" Fran yelled from behind me. I ignored her, treading carefully so as not to drop him, descending purposefully. I *had to* get outside. It didn't matter where we went, as long as it was out of her clutches. Fran gave a scream of sheer frustration, and I closed my eyes against the heat of her rage. It must hurt to realise her power over me had crumbled. That I was never again going to be the puppet she liked to control, the toy she used to work off her anger whenever she felt the desire.

How ironic that it had been *her* choices, *her* night of adultery that had started the chain of events that had given me the strength to finally stand up to her. If she'd stayed with me at Brett's party that night, maybe I'd still be begging and pleading and grovelling at her feet. But she'd broken the spell she held over me, and I would never be taken in by her again. I took another careful step as I moved down the stairs, and suddenly, I was overcome with a blinding pain as something crashed solidly into the back of my head. One moment I was paused on the middle step, the next, I was falling, the edges of my vision turning black, nothing but air beneath me as I lurched forward.

Instinctively, I twisted, curling my body inwards, my only thought being to protect the baby from harm. I landed on my back with a crash, hitting the floor hard, the smell of my own blood seeping into my nostrils. Eddie gave a surprised little cry that sounded like it was coming from far off in the distance, as if he were lost at the end of a long tunnel. And then, I felt myself losing the fight against unconsciousness. Everything went dark.

Chapter Thirty

Josh

I woke suddenly, gasping for breath as if I'd been trapped underwater, my thoughts racing as I clasped the empty space around me for the baby that wasn't there. I was on my back on the living room floor, though I had no recollection of how I'd got there. I sat up quickly, the blood rushing to my head, spots dancing before my eyes as I scanned the room for Eddie or Fran, finding myself very much alone. The curtains had been drawn tight, shutting out the daylight and a foreboding silence filled the room. A deep throbbing pain came from the back of my head and I knew without needing to touch it that whatever Fran had used to launch at me had done some serious damage.

With all my strength, I pulled myself to my feet, nausea hitting me hard as the room blurred around me. I had a concussion. I was certain of it. On shaking legs, I took unsteady steps towards the living room door and gripped the handle for support, pulling back. Nothing happened. I tried again. Nothing. It was locked, and from the feel of it, there was more than a flimsy padlock barricading my exit from the room. She'd made me a prisoner in my own home. Trapped me here so that I couldn't leave.

I strained my ears, listening for Eddie, hearing nothing. Where was he? Where had she taken him? I had to get out, I had to find him before they disappeared. I knew just how much satisfaction she would get from abducting him, punishing me with a pain that could never end. She would enjoy that.

I turned, making my way as quickly as I could manage towards the window, gripping the wall for support. I yanked back the curtain and gasped. No wonder it was dark in here. She'd boarded up the bloody windows from the outside. God, how long must I have been unconscious for her to do that? I glanced around, seeing the little battery operated clock on the bookshelf, squinting to read it from where I stood. I frowned and took a step closer, unable to understand what I was seeing. It read 23:07 and the date claimed it was the twenty-third of the month. But, it couldn't be, could it? That would mean it had been two days since Fran had attacked me on the stairs. *Two days?* She could have gone anywhere in the world in that time. I may never see her again. She could have taken Eddie *anywhere,* somewhere where nobody would question her, where she could get away with hurting him... or worse. There were places where she could do it, I was sure of it. Places she could tell the authorities that her baby had been abducted or taken ill and be believed. She could give him away and I would never get him back.

I spun, suddenly desperate, running back to the door, determined to break free, to get to my child, but my movement was too sudden. Black spots filled my vision and I felt myself lurch forward, my hands shooting out to break my fall. I landed hard, my wrist bending unnaturally to one side and I heard a loud crack as the pain shot through me. I curled onto my side, not needing to look down at my wrist to know that it was broken. The pain was too intense to mean anything else. How could I have been so stupid? How was I ever going to get out now? I let out a yell of pain, overcome with a sense of loss that pierced deep into my heart, wondering where my son was and if anyone was holding him right now.

I woke, finding myself in the same spot on the carpet, my wrist throbbing, shooting agonising spasms up the length of my arm. It was hard to even think of anything but the pain. I lifted it tentatively and saw how swollen it was. My mouth was as dry as sand and I realised there was no water, no food. If I stayed in this room much longer, I would die.

Was that what she had intended? Was she really so broken, so utterly intent on punishing me that she would leave me to die of dehydration? I glanced at the clock and saw that it was coming up to five in the morning. Almost six hours had passed since I'd lost consciousness again. I was a mess. I'd never felt so physically weak in my life. I was an absolute joke.

I pulled myself to my feet, relieved that at least for now, the black spots had stopped dancing in front of my eyes. That had to be a good sign. With slow, careful footsteps I walked to the light switch, flicking it on. Nothing happened. I tried the lamp on the side table, and then picked up the TV remote. Nothing. She'd turned off the electricity. I rattled the door handle again, then slammed my shoulder into it with all my might, ignoring the pain that shot through my limbs. The door didn't budge. I was trapped. Panic poured into my nervous system as I realised just how bad my situation was. I had to get help. I had to try.

Sucking in a deep breath, I flung back my head and yelled at the top of my voice. "Help! Somebody help me!" My head span and I lowered myself onto the floor, cradling my throbbing wrist against my chest as I sat back against the base of the armchair. "Help me!" I yelled again. "I'm trapped, please, someone help!" I bellowed. Remembering a snippet of knowledge I'd tucked away in the back of my mind, I sucked in a breath, and bellowed into the air. "Fire, fire, fire! Help, call 999! There's a fire here!" I screamed into the silence. People always came when there was a fire. It was what you were supposed to shout in an attack, or a rape case, simply because people were wired to investigate, they found the threat of fire impossible to ignore. There was a sudden noise outside the door and I let out the breath I'd been holding, relief flooding through me. "Is someone there?" I yelled. "I'm in here! Help me, please!"

A succession of clicks and clatters sounded, shuddering screeches like furniture being dragged across the wooden floor, and suddenly the living room door swung open, light flooding the room. I lifted my forearm to shield my eyes as I tried to focus on my saviour. A figure stepped into the room and I looked up in horror as I recognised it.

"Will you shut the fuck up?" Fran said, folding her arms tight across her chest. "I hope you've learned your lesson, Joshua? Or should I give you a few more days to think about it?"

Chapter Thirty-One

Josh

"Fran!" I yelled, scrambling to my feet. "What's going on? Where have you been?"

"Been? I've been here, waiting for you to come to your damn senses." She took a step into the room, pursing her lips in a tight line. "So, have you?"

My head swam as I tried to focus on her. "Have I what?"

She took another step closer and I glanced behind her, squinting. There was no sign or sound of the baby. I felt a sudden chilling sensation, like ice hardening around my heart, making it hard to even take a breath. I swallowed back my panic and fixed her with an unwavering stare. "Where is Eddie, Fran?" I said softly, my voice low and calculating.

I saw the way she paused, the unmistakable flicker as her eyes lowered to the ground before she regained her composure. It was a look I'd seen a thousand times over. The look she wore when she caught a glimpse of my bruises the morning after one of her rages and tried to pretend she hadn't seen. When she overheard me on the phone, fabricating lies for why I'd had to miss work because my injuries were too evident. *Guilt.* Seeing it now made my body spring into action, fear and adrenaline running through me. I took two steps towards her, grasping her shoulders with no fear for my own well-being, ignoring the sickening agony that shot through my shattered wrist.

I'd always been physically bigger, stronger more powerful than her. That had been what made our situation so shameful, so impossible to escape from. Who would ever have believed what she'd put me through when they looked at us side by side? But it had been her superior mental strength that had always kept me in my place. Her absolute certainty that she was smarter, that she could dominate me and that I should be grateful that she'd lowered herself enough to choose to be with somebody like me. I'd let her rule me because I didn't think I deserved more. And maybe she was right. But *Eddie* did. Maybe I couldn't fight for me, but I would fight to the death for him.

"Answer me," I said through gritted teeth. "What

have you done with my son?"

"You don't have a son... not anymore," she said softly. Her eyes wouldn't meet mine. "And neither do I."

"What the hell are you talking about?"

She gave a bitter laugh and screwed her face up. *"You.* That's what I'm talking about! You and your ridiculous plan to leave me. *You* did it, you stupid bastard!"

"Did it? What? What are you saying?"

Her face blanched and she finally met my eyes. "Killed him," she whispered. "When you fell. You landed on him, Josh, don't you remember?" She shook her head slowly, her eyes wide as she stared up at me. "You crushed the poor thing to death."

I stepped back, disgusted at her words. "Shut up! Don't you dare say that, it's not true!" I yelled, holding my hand out in front of me as if I could shield myself from her nightmarish accusation.

"It is. He's gone. I tried to save him, but I couldn't. He's gone."

"No! No he isn't! You're lying!" I yelled,

stumbling backwards. I hit my wrist against the wall and cried out, but the pain of my fractured bone was nothing now, not compared to this. I couldn't believe it. I wouldn't. I shook my head and pushed back from the wall, needing to see, to know for sure. I dashed past her, making for the stairs, taking them two at a time. The door to his nursery was open and I rushed through it, ripping the bedding off his cot, hoping to see him there, his face tear-stained but relieved as he held his arms up to me, demanding to be held. The empty mattress caused me physical pain, the sight of his little blue puppy teddy lying alone and unloved in its centre.

I turned and ran into the spare room, where Eddie and I had shared so many long nights, pulling the mattress out of the Moses basket, hauling it across the room in my grief, bellowing into the utterly empty room. He was gone. My baby was gone and I had missed my chance to save him. I turned, tears streaming down my cheeks, to find *her* standing there in the doorway. She stepped into the room, offering a tiny shrug. "We'll get through this," she said softly.

"As long as we're together, we can get through anything. We'll be okay. We really will." She stepped closer and I backed away, not through fear, but disgust. It had been her who had made this happen. She'd thrown something so hard at the back of my head, that I'd lost my balance and blacked out whilst carrying our precious child. The son she'd nurtured inside her own body for nine months. How could she possibly think I could stay now? Knowing who she was? What she was capable of?

"Did you call for help?" I whispered, my voice coming out in a croak. "Did you call for an ambulance?"

"It was too late. It wouldn't have made a difference."

"Where is he?" She shook her head, looking away. "Where did you put him? Where is he, Fran! I need to see him!"

"It's over, Josh. Forget it. He's gone."

"Forget it? Are you seriously telling me to forget it? You're unbelievable, do you know that?" I stared at her, hating her more than I'd ever hated anyone in my life, my absent father and sadistic mother included. I couldn't stay here, not a second longer. With a sudden, blinding clarity, I knew exactly what I needed to do. I pushed past her and ran back down the stairs, not daring to pause and give her another chance to attack me from behind as I ran into the kitchen.

I stopped in my tracks as I remembered the DNA test she'd threatened me with. Sliding my hand into my pocket, I pulled out the crumpled sheet of paper, and without stopping to think, I lit the gas on the hob, feeding the paper into the flame, watching it smoulder and burn with a sense of relief. I would not let my son go to the grave with doubt hovering over his paternity. I didn't care what the science said. What his biology claimed. Eddie had been my son since the moment I learned of his existence, and no piece of paper could ever convince me otherwise. I dropped the last smouldering corner into the sink, dousing it with cold water, watching the final pieces disappear down the plug hole.

With my one good hand, I picked up my jacket from the back of the breakfast bar stool, feeling the pocket to check for my wallet and keys. They were still there. A wave of dizziness hit me and I braced myself against the kitchen counter, sucking in deep steadying breaths. I couldn't let myself give into the pain, I had to stay conscious. I breathed in again, swallowing back the nausea.

Fran rushed into the kitchen behind me, pausing just inside the door, her hands shaking by her sides. She balled them into fists and crossed her arms, tucking them beneath her armpits to hide her weakness from me. Even now, she couldn't bear to be seen as vulnerable. "You can't leave. You have to stay here with me," she said, some of the usual bravado missing from her voice. She tried to sound in control, but I could tell she knew she'd pushed me too far. She'd crossed a line we could never come back from. "Where would you even go?" she asked.

I looked up at her, still bracing myself against the counter. "Go? Where do you think? I'm going to the police to tell them what we've done. What did you think, huh? That we could just keep pretending that nothing happened? That you didn't cause the fall that killed our child? I'm going to tell them the truth, Fran! I'm going to tell them everything."

"You can't!" she gasped, stepping closer, her trepidation replaced by the instant fury she never failed to surrender to. "Who killed him, Josh? Who crushed him to death? What do you think they'll say when they realise it took you more than two days to even report it? You'll be in as much trouble as me!"

"I don't care about that!" I yelled, stepping towards her, seeing the shock on her face as she realised I wasn't backing down. "I don't give a fuck what happens to me now! It doesn't matter, nothing matters now! It's over. This whole mess we called a relationship, *a marriage,*" I laughed, finally seeing the sick joke it had been from day one. I should have walked away after the house-fire with the twins. I should have realised then how deep her narcissism ran, to think *she* was more important that the life of that little girl. I met her eyes with absolute certainty. "It's finished, Franchesca, and the only good thing to come out of it, is that our poor baby won't have to grow up with you for his mother!" I pushed past her, not wanting to give her a chance to even respond as I strode out of the room, heading for the front door.

"Josh!" she screamed from behind me.

I caught a glint of silver and flinched, raising my arm instinctively as I span to face her. I heard the sound of laughter rising up from my own chest as I saw the kitchen knife clasped in her fist, the sharp tip pointing in my direction. "So you're going to kill me, are you?" I said, my voice incredulous. I felt nothing. No fear. No desire to plead and beg for her forgiveness, for the mercy that I already knew she wasn't capable of giving. I was numb. "So do it then. Kill me. Put a fucking end to this pain, because you know what? You already broke me beyond repair. I don't have anything left."

I dropped my jacket on the floor and stepped forward, holding my arms out wide. I saw the shock flash across her face, the realisation that her plan was going awry and I wasn't following the unspoken rules of our relationship. But still, the fear that should have been pulsing through my nervous-system didn't come. I wasn't afraid. And I wasn't bluffing. If she wanted to end my life it would be a relief. The first mercy she'd ever shown me, though I knew she wouldn't intend it that way.

She hesitated for a moment, then, slowly and purposefully, she spun the knife in her hand. She stepped forward, lifting her red silk blouse up to reveal her abdomen, pressing the tip of the knife into the wrinkled skin, still loose from stretching to accommodate Eddie. At the thought of his name, my heart froze in my chest, the pain almost suffocating. But I couldn't fall apart now. There would be time for that later.

"If you leave me, I'll kill myself."

I shook my head, bewildered. "Do you think I care? Do you think it makes any difference to me if you're dead?" I stared at her, wondering how she could possibly think this desperate attempt to bribe me could work. I took another step towards her, staring at her with all the hatred I'd stored up inside me, locked away for so long in a place I'd been unable to reach. It was free now, I'd opened Pandora's box and there was no way to go back. I lifted a finger, pointing to the knife, still pressed into her creamy skin. "Don't you realise? I'd do it myself if I were a stronger man," I spat, realising just how true the words were.

She shook her head slowly, a smug smile playing at the corners of her mouth. "I don't believe that, Josh. Are you really ready to lose your hero's crown? To have everyone believe you killed your wife *and* your baby?"

"Oh come off it, Fran! You're a joke, holding that knife to your belly like you'd actually hurt yourself. We both know the only person that matters to you is *you*. As if you'd do it. Even you're not that crazy, Fran. So, thanks for the amateur dramatics, but I don't have time for your games anymore." I bent down, picking up my jacket from the floor and heard a gasp. I looked up, my jaw dropping open as I watched her push the tip of the knife through her soft skin. I couldn't believe what I was seeing, it was like a nightmare, a horror movie playing out right there in my hallway. I froze, my arm stretching towards her, my jacket still grasped in my fist. "Fran! Stop, stop it!

What the hell are you doing?"

She stared down at the mess of blood spreading across her skin. The knife wasn't deep, I doubted she'd done any real damage. She was all about the shock value, but I'd never expected her to go this far. She raised her eyes to meet mine, and I saw the flash of victory in them. "Stay," she whispered. "Promise you'll never leave."

"Stay?" I shook my head. "Are you joking? Do you know what I feel for you now? I *hate* you. More than that. I despise you. Every time I look at you, I see *him*. Our sweet baby boy who you were too selfish to care for. Who you destroyed out of your own twisted jealousy. No, Fran, I wont stay."

"I didn't. I swear, I... I didn't, oh... Josh, wait, please!" She grasped the handle of the knife, pulling it out of her self-inflicted wound. My eyes widened in horror as I saw the blood spurt freely as the blade emerged. Fran's face blanched, the knife dropping to the floor as she grasped at her stomach, trying to stem the flow. There was so much blood. Too much. It spurted between her fingers, unrelenting.

"You... you must have nicked an artery," I breathed, my voice almost dreamlike as I watched the horrific scene unfold before me.

"Call for help... You need to call an ambulance!"

I shook my head, rooted to the spot, unable to tear my eyes away. She fell to her knees. Still I didn't move. Pulling her shirt over her head and balling it up, she pressed it hard against her skin. It made no difference. I could already see the silk turn sodden. Her eyes darted around in pure panic. It was a look I'd never seen on her face in all the time we'd been together. It was as if, after all this time, we'd exchanged our roles. Now *I* was the one in control and I was fascinated to find I had no more mercy for her than she'd had for me. Her gaze fixed on her phone, charging on the hallway table between us.

Slowly, with loud, breathless grunts, she crawled towards it, her determination to survive driving her on. I didn't think. I just moved, my legs carrying me forward, my hand reaching down, swooping her phone up and moving back towards the front door. "Yes, Josh, she croaked. "Call someone... Help me."

"I can't. I have to go." I almost said sorry, but the word stuck in my throat, and I was glad. I didn't want to offer her an apology she didn't deserve. I watched the realisation dawn in her eyes, then the callous hatred that had always simmered so close to the surface. She made an attempt to pull herself to her feet, but failed, lurching forward onto the floorboards, the soaked silk lying ruined beside her. I took a step back, slipped her phone into my pocket, then opened the front door with my good hand. "Goodbye, Franchesca," I said softly. I walked through the door, not daring to look back. I could hear her calling my name, but I didn't stop. I took a deep breath and kept walking.

Chapter Thirty-Two

Kaitlyn

"Thank you for agreeing to meet so early," I said, taking a seat in the chilly headmasters office, and stifling a yawn. I'd slept lightly last night after discovering that awful spray painted warning on my front door. It had taken hours to settle Rex to sleep, promising him he would be safe and that nobody was coming to hurt him. But despite my promises, I hadn't been able to convince myself that we were safe.

I'd woken at every tiny noise, sitting bolt upright in bed, my phone clasped tightly in my hand, ready to call for help. I hadn't even dared to turn out the light, sleeping with one eye open, waiting for monsters to emerge from hidden corners like a frightened little girl. When it came down to it, that was all I really was. I wanted my mother more than ever.

Mr. Clarkson feigned a smile and leaned forward, raising an eyebrow in response as I removed my coat to reveal my police uniform. I was sure I didn't imagine the way he straightened in his seat. I'd known it would work. "It's not a problem," he said silkily, "although we don't tend to arrange meetings for the morning. I am sure you can understand, this is rather a busy time for us," he added pointedly.

"I'm sure. But it was necessary. As I stated in my email, I am not prepared to leave my son in an environment where he isn't going to be safe. *Protected* from those who would hurt him. And so far, I'm sorry to say, I don't trust this to be the case."

Mr. Clarkson coughed, clearly surprised by my tone, but I didn't care. I had tried being nice. Pleading, appealing to his absent sense of charity. But he was no better than the students who went after my son. I knew from the glint in his eye when he talked about staffing shortages and stretched classes, how glad he was that a privileged woman like me had fallen so low. He liked that he could lord it over me, that I was at his mercy, and I knew he felt that Rex should learn the hard way how to fit in with his new peers. He'd told me as much to my face.

But I was done accepting that line. I was prepared

to do anything. To contact the papers, Ofsted, whatever it took to get this school to pay attention and do their duty to my child, and every other little boy and girl who was going through hell here, simply because they didn't fit in.

If it was demeaning, if my old friends from the life I'd lost saw my face plastered all over the tabloids, I wouldn't care, not if it saved Rex from any more pain. "I want to know what you're going to do for my son."

"Mrs... Sorry, *Miss* March. I know you're unhappy with certain aspects of the school, but it was wrong of you to keep Rex off without a valid reason yesterday. I will of course work with my staff to provide a safe environment for all of the children here, but you must do your duty too. I'm sure, being in the police yourself, you're more than aware of the law surrounding school attendance."

"I am. And I don't believe I've done anything wrong. So," I continued as he opened his mouth to interrupt. "I'll ask you again. What are your plans for keeping Rex safe from the children who have been bullying him?"

Mr. Clarkson sighed and I could see I was finally getting somewhere.

"It will be better. I told you, I've spoken to Mr. Clarkson and he's said you can choose any table to sit at in the classroom, and put your hand up at any time if you need to have a private word with Miss. Rogers. And you should," I said firmly. "If someone so much as calls you a mean name, I want you to tell a teacher right away. And at lunch, they're putting two extra staff on the playground who you can go to at any time if you're worried. They're going to talk to the parents of the boys you fought with tonight, and a letter will be going home to *all* parents about the school's firm stance against bullying. They want to make sure that every child knows that it won't be tolerated. It *will* be better from now on, Rex, I'm sure it will."

"I suppose," he sighed. We stopped on the outskirts of the tarmac playground and I saw the way he shrank into himself the closer we got to his classmates.

I'd had to drop him at Sarah's before seven to get to the meeting at his school, then I'd rushed back to collect him so I could bring him in myself. Marcus would be livid, but I couldn't think about that now.

I glanced at my watch, adrenaline pulsing through me. "I have to go now, sweetie, or I'll be in trouble with my boss. Remember what I said. Everyone knows to listen to you now and they're there to help if you need it." I pulled him into a tight hug and kissed the top of his head, breathing in the smell of him. "I love you," I whispered.

"You better let go," he replied. "I don't want anyone to see." He pulled back and I nodded, swallowing thickly to hide my hurt. I hated that he had to act a certain way, *be* something that he wasn't in order to fit in. It wasn't right.

"Well, I'll be off then, okay?"

"Fine."

"I love you," I repeated.

"Yeah." He turned away and walked towards the

school, his head bowed low as he submitted to his fate.

The conference room was already filling up for the morning brief when I arrived at the station, rushing in to take my place beside Laura, a fellow constable who would have been a good friend in another life. She was warm and funny and I always wished I could find the time to invite her out for a coffee or a glass of wine. But friendships were nothing but a distant memory for me now. Life since Mitch had upped and left, was about pure survival. There wasn't the time or the money for cafes and wine bars. I glanced down the table and sighed with relief. "Marcus not here yet?" I asked in a low voice.

"He's around, but he's not been in here yet. Don't worry, your secrets safe with me. Coffee?" she offered, sliding the pot in my direction.

"Yes, please."

"I haven't seen you in a while," she said as I poured myself a cup. "You've had your hands full with all of this," she said, gesturing to the table where photographs of Josh, Franchesca and their home were scattered, people talking in little groups before the meeting began, no doubt sharing what they'd found. The latest information to emerge was that the living room at the couple's home had been transformed into a mini Fort Knox in the days leading up to Franchesca's death. The windows boarded up and the door fitted with several locks and bolts.

I'd only learned the information when Marcus had text me last night, not wanting me to walk in blind to the meeting this morning. I was sure he'd been holding out sharing it with me, because he knew what I would think. That Franchesca Jones had been abusing her husband. The state of their living room made my theory even more likely and I knew that would piss Marcus off beyond measure. He just couldn't seem to get his head around the possibility that a woman could overpower a man, and I was beginning to realise that he was old fashioned and a tad chauvinistic when it came to his views on the opposite sex.

"Yeah, it's been a hectic few days," I said, taking a

sip of the strong black coffee, wincing as I swallowed the bitter liquid down.

"Do you... never mind," she said, shaking her head and looking down at the table.

"What?"

She took a breath and fixed me with a smile that looked oddly sympathetic. "I don't want you to think I'm jealous. Of course, I'd love to have been given the opportunity you've had this week. I think it's a given that the promotion is yours on a plate if you want it. But I'm happy for you. I know you would be for me, if our roles were reversed."

"Right..."

"But there's something you should know, Kait. Something I heard."

"What is it?"

"Do you know why Marcus chose you? For the Jones case?"

"No. I've been trying to figure it out. I mean, I thought we got on okay, we've always been friendly with each other. I thought that might be it, you know? Doing a friend a favour. But he's not been that nice to me this week and sometimes I feel like he doesn't even like me. So no. I have no idea what prompted him to pick me. What have you heard?"

She sighed and blushed. "I probably should have told you sooner, but you've been hard to catch alone. I heard him talking to Jack and Frank. Last week," she said, casting her eyes across the room to the two guys in their late twenties. I didn't know either of them well, but I'd heard enough of their conversations about the girls they taken home, to know we lived very different lifestyles. Outside of work they were free to party and spend their money, with no responsibilities to tie them down.

"So? What does that mean?"

"There's no easy way to tell you, but I'm pretty sure nobody else will, and I would want to know. Marcus fancies you, Kait. He told the guys that he'd do you a favour so you could do him one. Obviously, the Jones case hadn't come in then, but he planned to give you the cream of the jobs whatever we got. This one landed right in his lap at the perfect moment. Oh, and he mentioned the conference."

"In Birmingham?"

"Yeah. I won't go into detail, but he said if you got the promotion, you'd be expected to go. He was talking about tricking you into sharing a hotel room. Pretending they'd overbooked. Said you'd owe him big time for getting you out of the shithole you've been living in. Sorry," she said, seeing me flinch. She placed a hand on my arm which suddenly felt all cold and clammy. "I wish I didn't have to be the bearer of bad news. But you need to be prepared. He could have just been joking, but it really didn't sound like it. I shouldn't have even been listening, but when I heard your name I couldn't help it. I just... I mean, *I* would want to know if it were me."

"Yes."

"And you should still go to the interview tomorrow. Don't let him ruin this for you. Once you get the job, you can tell him where to go. Make sure he knows that it's strictly professional between the two of you. It's easier if you're prepared. He won't be able to catch you off guard." She offered a weak smile and I didn't know what to say. I felt as if the ground was falling from beneath me.

The sound of people collectively dragging their chairs, straightening up volleyed around the room and I looked up to see Marcus come in, his eyes scanning the room until they found mine. He grinned and I gave a short nod, before looking away. I couldn't believe how stupid I had been. Blinded by my desperation to break out of my hand to mouth situation and to finally be able to help Rex. Be the mother who could fix things, rather than the useless woman who sent him back to a school where I knew he wasn't learning and he wasn't happy. My desperation had made me naive. Ready to believe that Marcus had helped me out of the goodness of his heart, when I'd seen nothing of his personality to indicate that he would actually care about *my* little problems.

I'd been an idiot, and I knew, even if I got the Sergeant position he would never let me forget his role in my success. I could report him for sexual harassment. I could go through the stress of tribunal, but I'd witnessed it dozens of times myself and the result was never fair. Maybe it would be more tailored to the victim these days, but did I really have the emotional resources in me to take that risk? I didn't think so.

Marcus was talking, his voice droning monotonously on, managing to make the fascinating details of the case sound deathly dull. The baby was still missing. It was hard to believe that not one person had called in the last forty-eight hours to report even a sighting. Marcus was talking about the planned press release to go ahead this afternoon and as he spoke, his eyes flicked in my direction every few seconds.

Had he always looked at me like that? My stomach churned and I focused on my coffee, aware of Laura's concern pulsing around me. I wished I could write off what she'd told me as petty jealousy, but I couldn't. As soon as she'd said the words, I knew in the pit of my stomach that she was telling the truth. It made sense. So many little things he'd said and done, the lingering glances, the casual brushes of his hand, the way he would briefly place a palm on the base of my spine as we crossed the road. Little things I'd pretended to ignore because I couldn't afford to acknowledge them. It changed everything.

The door banged open and Marcus cut off mid-sentence as every eye in the room turned to see who'd made the racket. "Guv," the Sergeant called, breathlessly. "Just had the Coroner on the phone. Franchesca Jones wasn't murdered. They've determined it as suicide."

Chapter Thirty-Three

Kaitlyn

"I want to be the one to tell him."

"He's not off the hook yet," Marcus said, folding his arms. "We need to find that baby. And whether he killed her or not, we still don't have half the facts."

The forensics report had arrived moments after the post-mortem report, stating that the blood they had found in the living room belonged to Joshua Jones, not his wife or son. Despite their thorough search, there had been nothing to help us determine what had happened to the baby, a fact that was causing the entire team to scratch their heads.

"Maybe he'll be willing to talk now that he knows he's not in the frame for her murder?" I suggested, fixing my radio onto my belt. Marcus stepped in front of me, blocking the door. I glanced over his shoulder, wishing someone would come to his office for advice, a quick chat. How many times had I let myself be alone with him in here, never thinking about how Marcus was seeing me? Had I led him on? Given him any hint that I'd be up for more? *No.* Since Mitch, I'd not given a single thought to romance. *Relationships.* I didn't have time for drama, and if I had, I certainly wouldn't have chosen a man almost twice my age going through a nasty divorce, and with the personality of a rabid squirrel.

"I don't have time to come to the hospital with you, Kaitlyn. We're still going ahead with the press release. We *need* to find that baby."

I nodded. "They've said he'll be discharged later today, all things going well. Will we bring him back into custody?"

"I don't think we have a choice. We need to question him properly." He scratched his chin and fixed me with a piercing stare. "Kait, I know you've got yourself a bit of a soft spot for him, but don't overlook the facts, okay? We don't know what he did to that baby."

"No. We don't. Look, I'll go to the hospital now and I should be able to make it back for the press conference this afternoon. There's a chance he'll talk more there than he will here."

Marcus sighed. "Go then. Though if it were me, I'd let him stew until he got back here. You all set for tomorrow? The interview is at eleven, isn't it?"

I nodded. "As ready as I'll ever be."

"You'll do fine. You're miles ahead of the other candidates. And I shouldn't tell you this," he said conspiratorially, stepping forward to place a hand on my arm, "but I've put in a good word for you." He flashed me a wide smile, his moustache twitching above his yellowing teeth, then gave my arm a little squeeze.

I pulled back, stepping around him to the door. "Thanks, I appreciate it," I said, glancing over my shoulder.

He spun to watch me go. "No problem. You can buy me a drink sometime," he winked. I turned away, my skin crawling.

I was just pulling up outside the hospital when my phone rang. I grabbed it from the empty passenger seat and sighed, seeing Marcus's name flash across the screen. "Guv?" I answered, glancing through the windscreen towards the hospital.

"Kaitlyn, are you with him? Mr. Jones?"

"Not yet."

"Good." He paused. "You aren't going to believe the news we've just had."

Chapter Thirty-Four

Kaitlyn

He was sitting by the window, expressionless as he stared out towards the watery blue sky. "Mr. Jones?"

He looked up, recognition dawning on his face, but he didn't speak. I stepped inside the cramped room, pushing the door closed behind me. "I won't ask how you're feeling," I said, moving around the hospital bed, closer to where he sat. I leaned against the edge of the plastic coated mattress, wondering how to tell him the news. I could hardly believe it myself.

"Mr. Jones," I started. "When you first came into the station, you told my colleague that both your wife and son were dead. Why did you say that?"

He shook his head in confusion. "Because they are. Why else?"

"You saw them? The bodies?"

"I – no... what are you getting at?"

"Josh, you didn't kill your wife, did you?" He stared at me, his eyes filled with confusion. I took a deep breath. "We found out this morning that the cause of your wife's death was suicide. The angle of the blade and the finger-prints on the knife handle have confirmed this. I don't know why she did it, but I'm guessing you do. And whether you want to or not, we will be questioning you again on the events leading up to her death." Josh shrugged. "You don't seem worried by that?"

"Why would I be? It's not as if I have much to live for now, is it?"

"Well, that might not be true." I gripped the edge of the mattress. "Why did you tell us your son was dead, Josh?"

"What?"

"Edwin. Why did you report him as dead? We've had people out looking for a body."

"I – I don't understand what you're asking me?"

"I'm asking why you would fabricate a murder, when the baby is still very much alive?"

Josh moved so fast I didn't see him coming. In half a second he was out of his seat, his hands on my shoulders as he stared at my face with an intensity that shook me to my core. "What are you talking about?" he demanded. "What do you mean he's alive?"

"Mr. Jones, remove your hands from me right now, unless you want to finish this conversation in cuffs."

With what looked like a tremendous show of strength, he pulled back, his eyes never leaving mine as he took a step back from me. "Tell me. Please."

I nodded. "We received a call from a Mrs. Mathilda Payne earlier this morning," I said, pausing to see if there was a trace of recognition on his face. There was nothing. "She's a childminder, located a ten minute drive from your home. Mrs. Payne reported an abandoned child in her care, stating that a woman had contacted her for emergency childcare for a six week old baby earlier this week, begging her to take him because she needed to go to her dying father in Exeter and wouldn't be able to care for him herself. Mrs. Payne agreed to take him on short notice, but when the child wasn't collected last night, as arranged, she called the emergency telephone contacts she'd been given, only to discover they were false. She kept the baby overnight, then still unable to contact the mother, and with no valid address to take him to, she contacted us today." I paused, waiting for Josh to react.

"You aren't saying it's Eddie?"

"That's exactly what I'm saying. The forms the childminder has are for an Edwin Jones, born five weeks and six days ago, and the primary carer is listed as Franchesca Jones. The address is false, but it seems the mobile number is registered to your late wife, though it isn't switched on. Since you seem to be the only person who could identify him, I need you to tell us if we have the right child."

"You have him?" Josh breathed. "He's alive?" He looked around the room as if the baby could be hiding somewhere, his eyes wide, his mouth trembling. He took a step back, stumbling against the table leg, gripping the arm of the chair for support as he leaned forward taking deep shuddering breaths. "Where?" he asked, looking up at me. "Where is he?"

"He's here. With a nurse just outside. If you're

willing, I could bring him in now?"

Josh straightened up in an instant, running towards the door before I could stop him. He flung it open, rushing into the hall. The constable at the door gave a yell and I dashed after both of them, grabbing the officer by the sleeve as I watched Josh come to an abrupt halt in front of a nurse. She was cradling a tiny bundle in her arms and I saw the fear flash across her face as Josh reached forward. With slow, shaking fingers, he eased back the crochet blanket to see the baby's face. He mouthed something inaudible under his breath, then with a cry that made my blood tremble, he let out a shuddering sob and fell to his knees, his head leaning against the nurse's shins, his beefy hands gripping her sensible black shoes. I could hear him repeating the same words over and over again. "Thank you, thank you, thank you!"

Josh couldn't stop touching the baby's face as he stared down at him in wonder, tears flowing in a constant stream down his cheeks, his full lips pressed into a content smile, transforming his face from the sullen mask I'd always seen him wear. He looked like a man who'd just won the lottery. A man who'd been granted his every wish in one go. Marcus had joined us at the hospital having cancelled the press conference and we'd crammed back into Josh's hospital room so we could continue talking.

"So let me get this straight?" Marcus said, sitting down opposite Josh and Eddie. "Your wife told you that Edwin here was dead. But you didn't ever see him for yourself?"

"That's right," Josh answered. It was amazing to see the transformation in him now that he had his son back in his arms. He'd been a different man this past thirty minutes, answering every question we fired at him, happy to tell us whatever we wanted. It was as if someone had switched the life back on inside him.

"And why would you just believe her? You had no proof. Why take her word for it?"

"Because it could have been true. She told me that Edwin had died when I fell on him, after she attacked me on the stairs, and for all I knew, I could have done. She hit me so hard I couldn't stay conscious," he said, matter of factly. "You don't know what she was capable of. *I do.* And I knew she would never have called an ambulance, not when she was to blame. It was completely plausible to me that she would let Eddie die to prevent herself from facing the consequences. Like I told you, she had no love for him. She never cared for anyone but herself. It took me far too long to realise it."

"But why lie? What would she have to gain from it?"

"To hurt me," he answered simply. "Everything she did, was to cause me pain. I should have found the strength to leave a long time ago. Taken Eddie where she couldn't hurt us anymore..."

I stepped forward, touching his arm lightly and he glanced up at me. "It wasn't your fault, Josh. You can't let yourself think that way. You didn't deserve it. Nobody deserves to live in fear." He nodded and I suddenly pictured Rex as I'd dropped him off at school earlier. The way he'd walked bravely back towards the people who loved to hurt him for their own amusement. The fact that I'd been unable to protect him made me sick with guilt.

After Marcus had arrived at the hospital, Josh had bravely explained the source of his many injuries. The scars on his torso had been Franchesca's handiwork, but the cigarette burns on the soles of his feet, he'd confessed, had been there since his childhood. One of his mother's favourite ways to punish him, he'd told us through a veil of tears.

It wasn't fair, the way the women in his life had broken his trust, used his gentle nature to gain power over him. I was glad, at least, that Marcus could finally see how wrong he had been. Josh was as far from the typical picture of a victim of domestic abuse as you could imagine, but that hadn't stopped him from becoming one. I was blown away by his bravery now. I blinked fast and looked over at Marcus. "So what happens now? Franchesca's death has been ruled as suicide and little Eddie here is perfectly fine."

Marcus gave a short nod and looked at Josh. "You're free to go. You and your son. But next time, if there ever is one, please try and supply us with all of the facts so we don't end up on a wild goose chase.

Got it?"

"There won't be a next time," Josh said, smiling down at the baby. "When it comes to women, I think I've finally learned to recognise what to avoid." Josh stood carefully, propping the baby in a practised arm as he shook Marcus's hand, then mine. We watched him go and I smiled after him.

Marcus stepped behind me, his hand going to my shoulder. He spoke into my ear and I felt my muscles tighten apprehensively. "You did well this week, Kaitlyn. I think you and I are going to have a lot of fun working together."

I stepped forward, breaking free from his touch and glanced down at my watch. Rex would be back in class having finished his lunch break by now. "Actually, Marcus," I said, taking off my radio and handing it to him, "I really don't think we are."

Chapter Thirty-Five

Kaitlyn

The playground was silent as I jogged across it, buzzing into reception to be admitted inside the school. "I'm here to collect Rex March," I said as Mrs. Simms, the receptionist fixed me with a beady stare.

"Oh? For an appointment?"

"If you like." She frowned and walked around the desk, opening the main door. "Actually, I'll come with you," I said firmly, moving forward.

"Oh, we don't allow parents into the school during lesson time. It's disruptive."

"I'm coming in," I insisted.

She twisted her mouth. "Fine. I suppose I can't exactly threaten to call the police on you, can I?"

"No, I don't suppose you can."

"Go on then. You might as well go and get him yourself. You know where he is?"

"I do." I walked through the door, ignoring the exasperated tut she gave as I passed. The corridors in these places were always so much smaller than they seemed when you were small. I wandered past the murals of children's artwork, listening to the murmur of young voices and rumble of disapproving teachers reprimanding students. Rex's classroom was on the right and I paused just outside the window, trying to keep out of sight so I could observe him unnoticed.

He was sitting alone in the far corner of the room, his ankles crossed tightly, his hand gripping his pencil, though he wasn't writing. The little desk he sat at was the one reserved for disruptive children who needed to be separated from the others. He'd been allowed to choose any table to sit at, and *this* was where he'd decided on. Alone. Cut off from the others. His face was pale and sad as he stared down at his work, and I saw the way the other children laughed at him, the boy who threw a screwed up ball of paper at the back of his head. The whispers behind the backs of hands.

Miss Rogers couldn't have missed the underlying malice going on right under her nose, but she stood at the whiteboard, studiously ignoring the very thing she was supposed to address. It wasn't good enough. The school weren't willing to actually tackle the issue and they never would be. As long as they made the right noises, spouted the empty promises, they felt like they'd done their bit. They didn't actually care about Rex. They weren't invested in him. And it just wasn't good enough.

I opened the classroom door without knocking, and several children gasped, pointing up at me. One boy jumped up on his chair, yelling, "It's the mutha' fuckin' po – lice!" and I grimaced. Rex turned, his mouth dropping open when he saw it was me.

"Miss. March, what are you doing here?" Miss. Rogers said, folding her arms tightly across her chest.

I ignored her. "Come on, Rex. We're leaving. And you're never coming back." Rex's eyes grew wide, then his whole face lit up. He grabbed his pencil case and ran towards me, his hand sliding into mine.

"Fuckin' mummy's boy!" someone shouted across the classroom. Rex squeezed my hand tighter and I nodded reassuringly.

"Miss. March! What do you think you're doing?" Miss. Rogers exclaimed.

"Fancy some ice-cream, sweetie?" I said, leading him out of the classroom without bothering to offer an explanation to the gob-smacked teacher. I grabbed his backpack from the hook, noticing how someone had defaced the name label above it, so that it read Rex March *stinks of farts!* It didn't matter. Not anymore. We walked out onto the empty playground, the sun shining brightly above us.

"Am I really never going back there, Mummy?"

"Never ever. I'm sorry it took me so long to decide. I was just trying to do the best thing for you, darling. It's not always easy being a mummy. Sometimes we get it wrong."

"You're a great mummy. The best. Are we really getting ice-cream?"

"Of course. And there's more. You remember Grandma's cottage?"

"By the beach? In Welch?"

"Wales. That's right. In Pembrokeshire. Anyway..." I said, taking a deep breath. "What if we left London? Grandma said we could live with her for a little while, and there's a nice little school in the village, with lovely teachers, and you could play on the beach every day."

"And have ice-cream?"

"Every weekend!"

Rex looked up at me, his little forehead puckering. "But what about your new job, Mummy? Your special interview? Didn't you get it?"

I shrugged. "Actually, I realised I don't want it."

We crossed the road and I lead Rex through the little park to the kiosk that opened in the afternoons. I ordered a chocolate ice cream with a flake and hundreds and thousands, and pressed the cone into his hand, feeling more and more certain I'd made the right choice. We went to sit on a bench in the sunshine and I watched him eat, smiling. "I saw something today that made me realise what I *do* want," I said, thinking of Josh, the way his whole life had been gifted back to him in a matter of seconds.

"What, Mummy?" Rex asked, licking a dribble of chocolate from his sticky chin.

I smiled. "To be with you. To have much more time to spend with my favourite boy. And I want to spend more time with *my* mum too. I don't want to miss the important things. What do you say to that, Rex?"

He grinned and for the first time in as long as I could remember, he looked like a little boy again. He popped the last piece of cone in his mouth, chewing slowly, his face thoughtful. He swallowed and turned to me, his eyes sparkling with excitement. "When are we leaving?" he asked.

"How fast can you pack?" I laughed, wrapping him in a tight hug. This was the right thing to do. I could feel it, the certainty that spread through my body, the way my heartbeat stopped pounding with the frantic adrenaline it needed to produce to get me through the non stop days here, and slowed to a gentle rhythm. Going home to Wales had always seemed like admitting I'd failed. It had seemed impossible, and I'd never let myself acknowledge that it would make me happy. But now, having seen Josh get his son back, the joy in his eyes as he pictured their future together, it made everything so clear.

I didn't *want* to stay in London, a place where

everything reminded me of what I'd had and what I'd lost. I didn't want to work for a man like Marcus, send Rex to another school where there were too many students and not enough teachers. I wanted to go home, and I already knew we would be welcomed with open arms. I wanted to wake up to the sound of rain against my window, and go outside to breath the fresh sea air. To spend my free time building sandcastles with Rex and sharing a pot of tea with my mother, not buying more locks for my front door to keep the neighbours at bay. I didn't want this life anymore. I was ready to go home, and that was okay. I'd finally come to understand that sometimes, going backwards was the only way to move forwards.

I stood up, holding out a hand to Rex who jumped up instantly, his whole body loose and relaxed, the depressed slump of his young shoulders vanished. "Let's go and call Grandma and tell her the good news, shall we?"

His hand slipped inside mine and together we walked away from our old lives, towards something better.

Epilogue

Josh
Eighteen Months Later

"Dada! Swing!" Eddie called, his little bottom wiggling as he toddled across the unsteady woodchip.

"I'm coming, son, don't you worry." I dropped his little Fireman Sam backpack on the bench and jogged across the park, catching him up. The day was bright and warm and I stripped of Eddie's jumper before lifting him into the bucket swing. A little girl was kicking her legs high on the swing beside him, her grandmother pushing her with a vigour that was impressive. "How old is he?" the woman asked, as Eddie wriggled gleefully, his chubby legs kicking out as he imitated the little girl.

"Nineteen months," I smiled.

"He is the spitting image of you," she said, plucking the girl from the swing. "Beautiful smile. Really beautiful." The little girl dashed off in the direction of the slide, the grandmother following after her, and I smiled to myself. After Franchesca's funeral, I'd spent months in a state of fear, wondering if one day someone would realise the truth of Eddie's biology. That there would be a knock on the door and someone would be standing there, calling me a fraud and a fake, demanding I hand him over. But despite my terror, it had never happened.

Franchesca, disgusted by her pregnancy, had barely admitted it was happening to herself, let alone to the man who I referred to in my head as the sperm donor. And as the months passed and nobody came, I began to relax a little. But there had still been a sense of fear beneath the surface. What if he grew up to look nothing like Fran, or me? Would people guess the truth? Would they push for answers?

It had been a shock the first time someone had commented on his resemblance to me. The smile, the woman at the post office had said. *He has your smile.* I'd watched him then, desperate for it to be true, wondering if she was right. It was easy to convince myself it was all in my imagination. Just a flippant remark I'd taken to heart. But the more I looked, the more I saw it. Though his hair was a sandy blonde, unlike mine or his mother's, his nose was a little narrower, and his lips not quite as full, his smile was so much like mine it made my heart swell. His whole face lit up when he was happy, and as the months had passed, I'd come to realise we shared more than I'd dared to hope for.

His love of adventure. His fascination with emergency vehicles, his deep sense of empathy. Even at such a young age, I could see *that* more than anything. He would stop to rescue a snail he'd found on the path. He'd stroke my cheek and look deep into my eyes when he thought I was sad. He was naturally sweet and kind and loving. He shared so little with his mother, and I was grateful for that.

"Hey, adventurers!" a voice called across the park. I looked up and saw Rebecca walking towards us, two cardboard cups clasped in her hands. "Thought I'd find you two here," she said, holding out a coffee for me.

"Thanks," I said, taking a sip as she bent down, kissing Eddie's cheek. He giggled and she stood back, giving him room to swing higher. It had taken a long time for me to realise what was right in front of my face. *Rebecca.* I had honestly never even considered stepping past our friendship. I'd only had time for Fran. But Fran had known. She'd always insisted there was something between Rebecca and I. Perhaps she could see what we hadn't been able to. Because it turned out, she had been right.

It was so unlike my relationship with Franchesca, I hadn't even realised what was happening. Nothing like the fireworks we'd had from the very beginning. The explosive passion that made me willing to do anything, *be* anything to make it continue. No, this was something quite different. Something that had started so very slowly. A shoulder to cry on in the months after Fran's death. A walk in the park when Eddie wouldn't stop crying because he was cutting a tooth. A movie on a Friday night with the baby sleeping across our laps. A lingering look, a tentative kiss and then... only then, had I realised the truth. The depth of feeling simmering way down beneath the surface of our friendship. Far stronger, more robust than anything I'd ever felt before. It wasn't sparks of passion and heated rows. It was steady. Stable. Something I could learn to trust. Something so much better than what I'd had before.

We were taking it slow. Very slow. I still had so much fear about letting another person get close to me. But Rebecca was different from Fran. She listened, never turning it into a story about herself, never tiring of hearing the secrets I'd hidden from the world for so long. She just held my hand and listened, never judging, never turning away in disgust. And with every day, it got easier. I shared more of my past with her. She let me into her world. And we got closer.

I put my arm around her now, both of us watching Eddie as he opened his mouth, tasting the air on his tiny pink tongue. It had taken so long to get to this place, to understand what it meant to be happy. Content. To unfurl the knot of fear that lived within my belly and breathe easy. But I'd finally made it.

There had been so many times I'd thought I would die. So much shame that the women who were supposed to love me, could treat me so cruelly. But Eddie had helped me see the truth. It was never my fault. I didn't deserve what happened to me. And I would never ever accept that life again. Rebecca slipped her hand into mine and together we watched Eddie laughing, his tiny toes pointing towards the sky. *This* was happiness. I'd made it.

The End.

Do you want to read my novella *What You Never Knew* for free? Download your copy now from www.samvickery.com.

About This Story

If you've been reading my books for a while, you'll be amazed to hear that this novel was *not* written from the comfort of my bed in my tatty PJs, but at my desk in my office. It's been there waiting for me to use it for years, but I've never been able to get over my dislike of proper working spaces and the way they conjure up memories of enforced work at school. Until now!

At the end of my tether with my insomnia, I changed up my routine and my habits, waking up to an alarm before my children woke, writing at my desk and even (shock horror!) getting dressed before starting my writing day. And it's been *amazing*. I'm sleeping better than ever and getting far more done during the course of the day. Who knew?

The idea for *Where There's Smoke* came, in part, from watching a documentary about men who are secretly living in fear of their partners and experiencing domestic abuse. What hit me was that there seemed to be an added layer of shame for these male victims, in that they knew how society viewed them; weak, not a real man, in need of pulling themselves together. Society expects men to use their strength to protect themselves. But what's interesting about these kinds of abuse is that often, it's not about being physically stronger. It's about the mental dominance.

Which is why I wanted Josh to be big. In my head, Josh is the spitting image of Dwayne 'The Rock' Johnson. He's a gentle giant. There's no way he could be a victim. Except he is. Because despite his size, his physical ability, he isn't mentally strong. He's been abused all his life, learned to bow to the will of his mother, accept things that would make most people hold up their hands and walk away. He's been cowed out of his instinct to fight back. His spirit has been broken and he has no idea what a healthy, loving relationship with a woman should look like. So when he meets Franchesca, it almost feels like coming home. He accepts the bad with the good, because he's so desperate to be loved. *Wanted.* And somehow, as time passes, he finds himself just as trapped as he'd been with his mother. And we all know, it's not always simple to stand up and walk away. Especially when you feel you don't deserve better.

Where Josh's story spans years, Kaitlyn's is condensed down to just a few days, which made it a challenge to dig in to. I feel like we're meeting her at a major crossroads in her life, all her fears peaking at once, forcing her to finally make a change. I was in two minds about her walking away from her promotion interview, not wanting her choice to be viewed as weakness on her part.

If she'd stayed and fought for the job, taken Marcus to task and moved Rex to a new school, it would have been considered a success story. But I wanted to explore the idea that sometimes, success doesn't look how we expect it to. Sometimes, admitting you've taken the wrong path and backtracking to where you really want to be, is the bravest thing you can do. Success on paper doesn't trump happiness, and there's no shame in admitting you've changed your mind. It took Kaitlyn a long time to realise that and I love the choices she made in the end.

I hope that you've enjoyed reading this story, I would be very grateful if you could leave a review on Amazon for me as they really do make a huge difference to the success of my books, and help new readers to find me.

And if you want to be the first to know about the next book I release, pop over to www.samvickery.com and sign up for my free reader list where you'll get all the latest news and no spam!

Until next time,

Sam

Also By Sam Vickery

The Things You Cannot See

Chapter One

Megan

"Megan?" Nate's voice called through the crowd of Sunday shoppers. I ducked behind a bookshelf, peering around it to see where he was, spotting him a little way ahead of me, Toby wriggling in his arms as he wrangled the pram and strained his neck to look for me. I should have called out. Smiled and waved and dashed to catch up to him. Taken Toby from him and settled the meltdown I could see already brewing in the overtired toddler.

Instead, I stepped back, heading into one of the perfectly set up nooks, displaying the kind of bedroom you too could have if you bought the carefully thought out Ikea design. I moved through the bedroom scene slowly, my fingers grazing against a sheepskin throw, my flat black boots scuffing against the laminate. A young, giggling couple came hand in hand into the room, ignoring me completely as they climbed onto the bed, bouncing up and down to test the mattress, cracking private jokes. I felt like a peeping Tom. Like a stranger who'd snuck into their bedroom, waiting for them to arrive. I watched their happiness with a mixture of confusion, jealousy and resentment. The woman bent low, kissing the man slowly and I fought the desire to throw something at them. We were in a department store, not a bloody nightclub.

Silently, I ducked through an archway and walked through another bedroom setup, then another, every step taking me further from my family. I arrived at one which had a high backed armchair placed by the fake window, a glossy scene of a city skyline at dusk pasted on to the perspex to create the illusion of a view. Purple and orange streaks slid behind black silhouetted skyscrapers. I glanced behind me checking I was alone, then climbed into the chair tucking my legs beneath me, curling up as small as I could manage as I stared towards the backlit view. I didn't know what I was doing. Why everything seemed to have changed so suddenly and so very drastically.

Two weeks ago, I'd been the happiest woman on the planet. Thirty eight weeks pregnant with my second child, the gender a surprise, though everyone knew I was secretly dreaming of a girl. Nate was too, although he would never have admitted it. The pregnancy had been almost dreamlike in its smoothness. Three measly days of morning sickness right at the start, and even then I'd only felt a bit queasy and had to sit down for half an hour until it passed. I hadn't had any of the aches and pains I'd expected from my first time around.

With Toby, I'd struggled with back pain, waddling from place to place in grimacing slow motion as I neared my due date. He'd been just thirteen months old when we'd decided to try for a second baby, and when I'd seen those two little blue lines appear on the Tesco pregnancy test just three weeks later, I'd been nervous about how I would cope with a toddler to take care of along with the exhaustion of pregnancy. I had thought it would take longer to conceive. That we would have time to prepare. But my worry was needless. It had been easy every step of the way. No headaches. Nothing too extreme in the hormone department. Loads of energy. And the constant feeling that I was the luckiest woman in the world.

Seven days ago, I had given birth to a dark haired, brown eyed baby boy. His arrival into the world had been just as smooth as the rest. Three hours of active labour, twenty minutes of pushing. No tears. No drugs, no complications. The midwife had handed him to me, wrapped in the same blanket I'd been wrapped in as a newborn. I'd kept it safe all my life, through my school days, getting married, moving house, I'd never lost it. It had been the first thing we'd used to snuggle our first baby in moments after his birth, and now, our final child, Toby's baby brother, would finish the line. I could remember thinking that perhaps, after it had become too small to keep him warm, we would put it away for safe keeping, and one day I might pass it on to one of my sons for their own leap into fatherhood. One day I might walk into a room and see the sparkling, brand new eyes of my grandchild peering out from beneath the mint green lambswool. And its journey would continue.

Nate and I had shared a look when we'd seen it was another boy, a look that communicated a thousand words in the dim warmth of the birthing room. *It doesn't matter one bit. We're so lucky. He's exactly right for our family.* He was pink and perfect and we'd named him Milo. We'd both been nervous when Jane, Nate's mother, had brought Toby in to meet him. Ready to stave off any jealous rages and feelings of rejection he might have. But there had been none of that. Toby had loved him instantly, had laid beside him, stroking his soft downy cheek with a look of reverence, his voice soft as he told Milo in his babbling, lispy voice that he was his big brother and that he would be so kind to him *foo evah*. Forever. It had seemed so strange to see my baby boy, my firstborn already taking on the responsibility of his new role. And for a few days, it had felt as if all of my wishes had been granted.

Now though, I couldn't stop myself from replaying that old proverb my grandmother always used to tell me. *Be careful what you wish for, it might just happen.* I'd never understood what she meant. It sounded like pure nonsense, like the one my mum used to say when I was sulky. *Megan, don't you know, I want doesn't get?* What was the point in getting something if you didn't want it? Pointless gibberish. But now, I was beginning to feel like I knew exactly what my grandmother had meant. Because, something was wrong. Horribly wrong. And nobody but me seemed to be able to see it.

When we'd come to this very store just a month previously to buy a new changing mat and eat Swedish meatballs and choose candle holders we didn't need, picking up cake cases in rainbow silicone, I had pictured coming back next time, light and free, without the pregnant belly to block my progress through the aisles. I'd imagined how I would walk as a mother to two children. How I would smile confidently as I meandered through the store, a tiny newborn held close to my chest as Nate and Toby dashed around opening drawers and cupboards, climbing inside them to jump out at me with wide grins on their faces. I'd thought this life was what I wanted. I'd been so sure. But I'd been wrong. I wished I could have known then what I knew now. I would have drugged myself. Poisoned. Thrown myself in front of a truck. *Anything* to stop this baby being born. Because he shouldn't be here. I'd made a mistake and now everything was going to change.

"There you are," came a deep, male voice from above me. Nate was looking down at me with concern in his hazel eyes, one hand on the pram handle as Toby ran to the bed, scrambling to get up on it. There was a high pitched keening coming from the depths of the pram, a wail of pure desperation. "He's hungry," Nate said, pulling the wheels closer, running his fingers through his messy brown hair. There was something pink and crusty on the collar of his sky blue shirt, and he looked ready to throw in the towel. This had been such a bad idea. "We couldn't find you, are you okay?" he asked, pushing the pram back and forth quicker now, his determined rocking having absolutely no effect on the unbearable noise coming from within. I nodded, though I was anything but. Nate put his free hand on my shoulder, squeezing lightly. "Is it too soon to be out? We can go back home. You can go and lie down in bed."

"Yes," I agreed, the word coming out in a whoosh of relief. "Let's go back. I'm tired." I stood up, walking past Nate, heading for the exit.

"Megan?"

I spun around, raising an eyebrow in question. "What?"

"You need to feed him first. The poor little fella is starving."

"Oh... oh, of course." I took a step back towards him, approaching the sound of the screams with caution. With shaking fingers, I pushed back the hood of the pram and stared down into the dark interior. I knew what I was expected to do. And I knew that if I told Nate the truth, he would laugh at me. He would never believe me. Never understand. The cries slowed as I lowered my head and Milo saw me, a halting, shaky sob shuddering from his throat as I reached for him and put him to my breast. Nate guided me back to the chair, handing me a muslin to mop up the dribbles. The baby fed ferociously, every draw of his small little mouth creating painful spasms right through my breast. It had never hurt with Toby. It had never felt so unnatural.

"There, that's much better," Nate smiled, catching Toby as he bounced from the bed. He carried him across to where I sat and the two of them smiled down at me. "See Tobes, he's fine now. All he wanted was his mummy."

I stared down at the baby, finally meeting his eyes as he released his mouth from me. He stared up at my face and I wondered what he was thinking. I let my gaze slide away from his. Then I stood up, placing him back in the pram out of sight, taking Toby from Nate's arms and heading for the exit.

The Things You Cannot See is available worldwide on Amazon Kindle, Kindle Unlimited and Paperback.

Also From Sam Vickery

Keep It Secret

Chapter One

There was a dead body on my kitchen floor. My mind should have been spinning, panicked, and yet it was more quiet than it had ever been. I glanced at the ticking clock, realising that Sophie must be getting hungry by now, it was past her dinner time. Straining my ears, I heard the comforting sounds of her singing to her dolls, the sweet lullaby of a girl who was made for motherhood, a child who has learned to nurture in spite of her own experience. She wouldn't come down until I called her. Even after two years, I knew she couldn't let go of those ingrained habits. She would wait, quietly, patiently, until she knew I was ready for her.

I looked at the motionless form sprawled on his back across the once sparkling white tiles, a pool of blood collecting in the creases of his arms, beneath his neck. He was wearing a thick gold chain that looked almost comical on his skinny frame, like some sort of cartoon gangster, and there was a tattoo of a skull peeking out from beneath the crusting blood that ran across his scrawny bicep. I twisted my mouth, staring at him, my eyes travelling over the brownish red puddle on my floor. I hoped it wouldn't leave a stain.

The thought struck me as cold, heartless and I shivered, the shock seeming to hit me all at once. Just a few hours before, I had been picking Sophie up from the school gates, my arms wrapping around her small waist, her hand slipping into mine as her words rushed out, telling me all about who she'd played with at lunch, the drawing she'd done of a baby elephant which she'd decorated with real leaves and grass collected from the school field. We'd stopped at the park on the way home, laughing as we'd swung side by side, challenging each other to go higher until it had felt like we were flying.

And now... now I had a body in my house. Blood on my floor. The bile rose in my throat before I knew it was coming. I span, grasping for the counter, heaving blindly into the chunky ceramic of the Belfast sink until there was nothing left inside me. Disgusted with myself for losing control, I rinsed away the evidence of my shock, letting the tap run boiling hot until the sink was clean. I straightened up, grabbing a bottle of bleach from the cupboard, pouring it liberally into the basin, scrubbing and rinsing until I could no longer smell the contents of my stomach.

I glanced at the pool of blood, wondering briefly if I should clean it now too, but I shook the thought away. That would make it look like I'd tampered with evidence. Like I was trying to cover up what I'd done. Hide something. It would look like a murder scene, and that was not something I could risk. I would have to be patient, difficult as it may be. The metallic smell of blood was strong enough to break through the fumes of the bleach and I was itching to pick up a cloth.

I dragged my eyes away from the body as I strode past it into the hall, my heels clicking against the tiles as I looked straight ahead. I dipped my hand inside my deep leather handbag, fumbling around before yanking out my lipstick, reapplying it with shaking hands in the hallway mirror. It was only then that I saw it. A streak of claret smeared across my forearm, the edges already flaking and brown. My stomach lurched heavily again, but this time I managed to swallow down my disgust. I took a breath, and then another, meeting my reflection in the mirror. "Get a grip, Isabel. Sophie needs you to be strong." I stared back at myself seeing the determination in my bright green eyes, the hard set of my mouth as I prepared to do what was necessary. And then I picked up my mobile phone and dialled 999.

Keep It Secret is available worldwide on Amazon Kindle, Kindle Unlimited and Paperback.

Printed in Great Britain
by Amazon

33898498R00201